Kaye Gibbons'

ELLEN FOSTER

"A captivating, often hilarious mix of Victorian fairy tale and fresh American lingo, told by an eleven-year-old orphan driven to desperation by the wickedest relatives in literature since King Lear. She enchants the reader in a style primitive, saucy and exhilarating."

—ALFRED KAZIN

"Filled with lively humor, compassion, and integrity . . . Ellen Foster may be the most trustworthy character in recent fiction."
—ALICE HOFFMAN, *The New York Times Book Review*

"Original, compelling, and frighteningly real, the voice of Ellen Foster makes the reader know her story in her own terms. Kaye Gibbons is a new writer of great force. She knows how to speak to our hearts."

—ELIZABETH SPENCER

ELLEN FOSTER

ELLEN FOSTER

Kaye Gibbons

Vintage Contemporaries

VINTAGE BOOKS   A DIVISION OF RANDOM HOUSE
NEW YORK

First Vintage Contemporaries Edition, May 1988

Copyright © 1987 by Kaye Gibbons

Library of Congress Cataloging-in-Publication Data
Gibbons, Kaye, 1960–
Ellen Foster.
(Vintage contemporaries)
I. Title.
PS3557.I13917E4   1988   813'.54   87-45936
ISBN 0-394-75757-2 (pbk.)

Author photo copyright © 1988 by Jerry Bauer

Designed by Marysarah Quinn

Manufactured in the United States of America
10 9 8 7 6 5 4 3 2 1

To My Sister, Alice,
And in Memory of Our Mother, Shine—
With Love, Respect, and Thanksgiving.

Cast the bantling on the rocks,
Suckle him with the she-wolf's teat,
Wintered with the hawk and fox,
Power and speed be hands and feet.

Inscription to "Self-Reliance"
RALPH WALDO EMERSON

ELLEN FOSTER

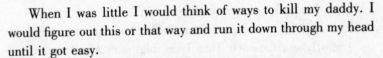

1

When I was little I would think of ways to kill my daddy. I would figure out this or that way and run it down through my head until it got easy.

The way I liked best was letting go a poisonous spider in his bed. It would bite him and he'd be dead and swollen up and I would shudder to find him so. Of course I would call the rescue squad and tell them to come quick something's the matter with my daddy. When they come in the house I'm all in a state of shock and just don't know how to act what with two colored boys heaving my dead daddy onto a roller cot. I just stand in the door and look like I'm shaking all over.

But I did not kill my daddy. He drank his own self to death the year after the County moved me out. I heard how they found him shut up in the house dead and everything. Next thing I know he's in the ground and the house is rented out to a family of four.

All I did was wish him dead real hard every now and then. And I can say for a fact that I am better off now than when he was alive.

I live in a clean brick house and mostly I am left to myself. When I start to carry an odor I take a bath and folks tell me how sweet I look.

There is a plenty to eat here and if we run out of something we just go to the store and get some more. I had me a egg sandwich for breakfast, mayonnaise on both sides. And I may fix me another one for lunch.

Two years ago I did not have much of anything. Not that I live in the lap of luxury now but I am proud for the schoolbus to pick me up here every morning. My stylish well-groomed self standing in the front yard with the grass green and the hedge bushes square.

I figure I made out pretty good considering the rest of my family is either dead or crazy.

Every Tuesday a man comes and gets me out of social studies and we go to a room and talk about it all.

Last week he spread out pictures of flat bats for me to comment on. I mostly saw flat bats. Then I saw big holes a body could fall right into. Big black deep holes through the table and the floor. And then he took off his glasses and screwed his face up to mine and tells me I'm scared.

I used to be but I am not now is what I told him. I might get a little nervous but I am never scared.

Oh but I do remember when I was scared. Everything was so wrong like somebody had knocked something loose and my family was shaking itself to death. Some wild ride broke and the one in charge strolled off and let us spin and shake and fly off the rail. And they both died tired of the wild crazy spinning and wore out and sick. Now you tell me if that is not a fine style to die in. She sick and he drunk with the moving. They finally gave in to the motion and let the wind take them from here to there.

Even my mama's skin looked tired of holding in her weak self. She would prop herself up by the refrigerator and watch my daddy

2

go round the table swearing at all who did him wrong. She looked all sad in her face like it was all her fault.

She could not help getting sick but nobody made her marry him. You see when she was my size she had romantic fever I think it is called and since then she has not had a good heart.

She comes home from the hospital sometimes. If I was her I would stay there. All laid up in the air conditioning with folks patting your head and bringing you fruit baskets.

Oh no. She comes in and he lets into her right away. Carrying on. Set up in his E-Z lounger like he is King for a Day. You bring me this or that he might say.

She comes in the door and he asks about supper right off. What does she have planned? he wants to know. Wouldn't he like to know what I myself have planned? She would look at him square in the face but not at his eyes or mouth but at his whole face and the ugliness getting out through the front. On he goes about supper and how come weeds are growed up in the yard. More like a big mean baby than a grown man.

I got her suitcase in my hand and I carry it to the bedroom. But while I walk I listen to him and to her not saying a word back to him. She stands between his mean highness and the television set looking at him make words at her.

Big wind-up toy of a man. He is just too sorry to talk back to even if he is my daddy. And she is too limp and too sore to get up the breath to push the words out to stop it all. She just stands there and lets him work out his evil on her.

Get in the kitchen and fix me something to eat. I had to cook the whole time you was gone, he tells her.

And that was some lie he made up. Cook for his own self. Ha. If I did not feed us both we had to go into town and get take-out chicken. I myself was looking forward to something fit to eat but I was not about to say anything.

If anybody had asked me what to do I would have told us both to feed on hoop cheese and crackers. Somebody operated on needs to stay in the bed without some husband on their back all the time. But she does not go on to the bedroom but turns right back around and goes to the kitchen. What can I do but go and reach the tall things for her? I set that dinner table and like to take a notion to spit on his fork.

Nobody yells after anybody to do this or that here.

My new mama lays out the food and we all take a turn to dish it out. Then we eat and have a good time. Toast or biscuits with anything you please. Eggs any style. Corn cut off the cob the same day we eat it. I keep my elbows off the table and wipe my mouth like a lady. Nobody barks, farts, or feeds the dogs under the table here. When everybody is done eating my new mama puts the dishes in a thing, shuts the door, cuts it on, and Wa-La they are clean.

My mama does not say a word about being tired or sore. She did ask who kept everything so clean and he took the credit. I do not know who he thinks he fooled. I knew he lied and my mama did too. She just asked to be saying something.

Mama puts the food out on the table and he wants to know what am I staring at. At you humped over your plate like one of us is about to snatch it from you. You old hog. But I do not say it.

Why don't you eat? he wants to know.

I don't have a appetite, I say back.

Well, you better eat. Your mama looks like this might be her last supper.

He is so sure he's funny that he laughs at his own self.

All the time I look at him and at her and try to figure out why he hates her so bad. When he is not looking I give him the evil eye. And my mama looks like she could crawl under the table and cry.

We leave his nasty self at that table and go to bed. She is sore all up through her chest and bruised up the neck. It makes me want to turn my head.

We peel her dress off over the head and slip on something loose to sleep in. I help her get herself laid in the bed and then I slide in beside her. She just turns her head into the pillow.

I will stay here with you. Just for a nap I will stay here with you.

Now at my new mama's I lay up late in the day and watch the rain fall outside. Not one thing is pressing on me to get done here.

I have a bag of candy to eat on. One piece at a time. Make it last. All I got left to do is eat supper and wash myself.

Look around my room. It is so nice.

When I accumulate enough money I plan to get some colored glass things that you dangle from the window glass. I lay here and feature how that would look. I already got pink checkerboard curtains with dingleballs around the edges. My new mama sewed them for me. She also sewed matching sacks that I cram my pillows into every morning.

Everything matches. It is all so neat and clean.

When I finish laying here with these malted milk balls I will smooth the covers down and generally clean up after myself. Maybe then I will play with the other people. But I might just lay here until the chicken frying smells ready to eat.

I do not know if she hears him go out the back door. She is still enough to be asleep. He goes off in the truck like he has some business to tend to. And you know and I know he's gone to get himself something to drink. Then he brings it into this house like

5

he is Santa Claus. He sets his package beside his chair and then eases his lazy self into place. Yelling at somebody, meaning myself, to turn on the television set. I could chew nails and spit tacks.

The yelling makes my mama jump and if she was asleep she is awake now. Grits her teeth every time he calls out damn this or that. The more he drinks the less sense he makes.

By the time the dog races come on he's stretched out on the bathroom floor and can't get up. I know I need to go in there and poke him. Same thing every Saturday. This week in particular she does not need to find some daddy hog rooted all up against the toilet stool.

I get up and go in there and tell him to get up that folks got to come in here and do their business. He can go lay in the truck.

He just grunts and grabs at my ankle and misses.

Get on up I say again to him. You got to be firm when he is like this. He'd lay there and rot if I let him so I nudge him with my foot. I will not touch my hands to him. Makes me want to heave my own self seeing him pull himself up on the sink. He zigs-zags out through the living room and I guess he makes it out the door. I don't hear him fall down the steps.

And where did she come from? Standing in the door looking at it all.

Get back in the bed, I say to my mama.

Mama's easy to tend to. She goes back in the bedroom. Not a bit of trouble. Just stiff and hard to move around. I get her back in the bed and tell her he's outside for the night. She starts to whimper and I say it is no reason to cry. But she will wear herself out crying.

I ought to lock him out.

A grown man that should be bringing her food to nibble on and books to look at. No but he is taking care of his own self tonight. Just like she is not sick or kin to him.

ELLEN FOSTER

A storm is coming up. And I will lay here with my mama until I see her chest rise up and sink down regular. Deep and regular and far away from the man in the truck.

I can smell the storm and see the air thick with the rain coming.

He will sleep through the thunder and rain. And oh how I have my rage and desire for the lightning to come and strike a vengeance on him. But I do not control the clouds or the thunder.

And the way the Lord moves is his business.

2

When it is morning I hear my daddy come in the house. He does not sneak. If he had a horse he would have ridden it right up the steps. He has forgotten last night and he is foolish enough to think we have too.

My mama has got her own self out of the bed. I must have slept hard not to hear her. All my clothes are on that I wore yesterday. It will save me some trouble this morning.

He's got her in the kitchen by herself. I know he won't hurt her with his hands. He might throw a cup or a fork at her but he won't touch her to leave a mark.

I try not to leave her by herself with him. Not even when they are both asleep in the bed. My baby crib is still up in their bedroom so when I hear them at night I throw a fit and will not stop until I can sleep in the baby bed. He will think twice when I am around.

And I have to see now but the door is shut. There is something in the kitchen I need so I go in there to get it.

She is sitting at one end of the table and he is sitting at the other end going through her pocketbook. Some of her heart pills are on the table rolling around loose and the bottle is in her lap.

Give the bottle to me and let me put the pills back in it. They cost money, I say to her.

That's all the pills she's got left. She took almost the whole goddamn bottle, he looks at her and tells me.

Vomit them up, mama. I'll stick my finger down your throat and you can vomit them up. She looks at me and I see she will not vomit. She will not move.

Well I'll just go to the store and use the telephone.

But my daddy says he will kill me if I try to leave this house. All the time I knew he was evil and I did not have the proof.

He would kill me and my mama both with a knife. He looks at the two of us and rubs her pocketbook, patient, like he sits and waits for folks to die all the time. He wants me to put her back in the bed.

Hell, all she needs is some sleep, he says. Take her back there and see if she don't sleep it off. And he gave me a guarantee the pills would not hurt her bad.

We will rest some more. The day is early and we need some more rest.

I always love to eat a good supper, brush my teeth and go to bed early. If I am not sleepy I can always find something to do.

Lately I lay up in the bed and read old books. I told the library teacher I wanted to read everything of some count so she made me a list. That was two years ago and I'm up to the Brontë sisters now. I do not read comic books or the newspaper. I find out what news I need off the television.

I can hardly tolerate the stories we read for school. Cindy or Lou with the dog or cat. Always setting out on some adventure. They might meet a bandit or they might hop a freight but the policeman or the engineer always brings them home and they are still good children.

I myself prefer the old stories. When I started my project I enjoyed the laughing Middle Ages lady that wore red boots. She was on a trip with a group of people swapping stories, carrying on, slapping each other on the back.

What I am reading now is a little fancy for me but it is on the list. Just men and women sneaking around in a big dark house with one all into the other's business. The library teacher said the author and her sisters wrote books because in their day they could not go out and get jobs. I bet they were just well off and did not need to work.

I could lay here and read all night. I am not able to fall asleep without reading. You have that time when your brain has nothing constructive to do so it rambles. I fool my brain out of that by making it read until it shuts off. I just think it is best to do something right up until you fall asleep.

I always want to lay here. And she moves her arm up and I push my head down by her side. And I will crawl in and make room for myself. My heart can be the one that beats.

And hers has stopped.

Damn him to the bottom of hell damn him.

What to do now when the spinning starts people will come and they will want to know why and I cannot tell them why. They will not come yet no not for a while. I have her now while she sleeps but just is not breathing. I do not have to tell him so let him sit and wonder at the quiet in here. Why this house is so still and people all over everywhere are glad for the day.

Guilty and held down in his chair by God and fear of a sweet dead woman.

You can rest with me until somebody comes to get you. We will not say anything. We can rest.

I despise that dress and get your hands off me is what she needs to be told. But I push the bathroom door and leave my aunt on the other side and me to myself.

Is this my lipstick now? I do not think I should put a dab on to wear to the church. She would let me. But somebody would say something.

Put it back put it back just like it was. When I am old I can come back and wear it. When it is not for play. They didn't need this to dress her up with? Somebody must have got her another stick. She left this one at home. To be sure they don't paint everybody they do business with with the same stick.

I will just wash my mouth and sit on the toilet to look. I can see them all through the crack in the door. Everybody I have not seen since last Christmas sitting around patting their hands together.

My daddy is thinking about how good a tall glass of anything would be. Before they all got here he rounded up all his beer cans and pitched them under the back porch.

Somebody must have given him that suit. All he ever wears is gray work outfits. I want to sew a little patch over the pockets that says his name BILL. He could be like the Esso man. Can I help you, ma'am? Check your tires? Change your oil? Throw a knife at you?

All he has done since Sunday morning is open the door for folks and shake his head yes or no. His brother Rudolph put him in the car and took him to town to pick out the coffin. I know when he got there my mama's sisters chased him off. They are the ones with the taste.

He sits there with both feet on the floor and his eyes are red but not from crying. When somebody goes by and leans forward to his ear he touches them on the shoulder. Still king. Now quiet.

She finally shut him up.

3

Oh I wake up and have the day and what do I want to do with it? I will go catch a pony and ride it. I can take something for me and the pony to eat in a bag so I can stay gone all day. I might get Jo Jo to ride with me. But I think she has ballerina lessons today.

I myself can dance.

I need to get up and eat what I smell. The oven door squeaks and she's holding soft round biscuits.

I got the clothes that I wore yesterday at the foot of the bed so I can change under the covers. It is not necessary to be cold so early. Just so my underwear is clean is all I care about today. By supper I will smell like pony all over.

Maybe nobody else has thought about riding that pony Dolphin today. One thing about here is that you have to wait your go. Today is my turn if I am the first one to get to the breakfast table.

My hair will smooth down without a comb. I look good as long as you don't see me from the back.

I feel good at the table with the biscuits. All that is cold is my hands. I hold them over the biscuit tin until my new mama tells me in a nice way that I am rude. So I sit on my hands until the biscuits are cool enough to hold. The others come in one by one or two but they see I was here first and will get the first biscuit and the pony.

I do not want to watch them anymore. What one can hardly wait to say to the other is making them squirm.

What did you expect? Marry trash and see what comes of you. I could have told anybody.

Here I am wearing this red checked suit like a little fool. When the day's over I'll burn it. I know my aunt Nadine wants to come back in here and fix me up. She gave me this outfit like she bought it just for me but I saw her girl Dora get her school picture taken in it last week. I do not have much choice but to wear it. In a while I'll be grown out of my underwear.

But that is OK by me. Just do not let that woman knock on the door and ask me how am I getting along in here. I ought to stuff my front and walk out with a sudden big chest. Give them something to see and discuss. Not just speculation.

Dora's mama thinks it is time to get this show on the road. She could not organize a two-car colored funeral so she has herself all worked up over this affair.

Stick the fruit delight and the food that'll go to the bad in the fridge. Fridge she says.

She's moving my way. I tell her I was just on my way out when she gets here. She will need a little privacy to adjust her slip and face. She wants to look especially good because she has elected herself to ride in the big car.

Oh yes and now we are all ready. My daddy wonders if I

14

plan to tell somebody the whole story. I do not know if there is a written down rule against what he did but if it is not a crime it must be a sin. It is one way or the other. And he wants to know if I'm telling.

My aunt sashays her large self out of the toilet and I suppose now we line up to go. She must have gone to school to learn how to get grown folks into little bunches and decide who rides behind who.

Won't she be disappointed when we get there and they put her away and we come home and that is all? She will go back to her house tired but not too tired to think about how smoothly everything went.

You are definitely in the first car, she tells me. Just so I got a ride there is all.

The undertaker opens the car door for me. He has been to the house twice since Sunday just to say he cares. I am glad he cares but I think I would like him better if he said it is my job to care. I make more money than you will ever see just to care. That would not offend me.

I do hate to sit in between folks in a car. Put me by the window so I can get some air and get out quick if I need to. I demand to ride by the window in this car that is big enough to hold the smiling undertaker, Dora's mama, Dora, my daddy, and me.

The other children know the pony is not specifically mine but they let me play like he is mine.

After I eat all I can hold I ask for some maybe just two more biscuits to take with me please. The pony and me would both enjoy a biscuit with some fried meat and jelly. That is what we will eat for lunch. I have my thermos and my sack ready to fill up.

I keep calling things mine but nothing actually belongs to me except a few things that I moved out here with. But while you use or play with the things here it is OK to call it yours. When you get through with something, clean it up and put it back so the next one can call it his. That is the rule.

I have my lunch and I am dressed warm and ready to go.

And away I leave the house and my new mama standing at the kitchen window watching me run across the yard to the pasture.

I need to roll down the car window and stick out my face. Dora is used to her mama's scent and my daddy is past smelling. The smiling man is too kind to remark.

He just drives slow down the path dodging the holes and the wide washed-out places. He will need to wash this big car before he picks up the next load of strangers.

When I get out I want to count the tires.

Having sidled herself up beside the smiling man, Dora's mama searches for just the right thing to say. The man will think how wonderful she is and maybe find a job for her.

What a lovely day! She decides on this.

And I look at the back of her neck and think to myself my mama is dead in the church, my daddy is a monster, your girl is probably going to pee on me before this ride is over and that is all you can find to say.

I just see out the window all the folks' houses and barns and dogs running in the yards. You cannot help but notice everything because he drives so slow.

The leaves are starting to change good. Every year I want all the leaves to be fall-colored at the same time but there are always some that don't match.

I know this is the best time of the year. The leaves and people too changing and doing things to get ready. I like to read about men and their boys who tap maple trees in New England. They wear plaid jackets and hats with ear flaps when they go to the woods to get the syrup. It does not get cold enough to do that here even in January.

That tree in Junior's yard is redder than it was yesterday. When it looks so red it could explode on fire and burn down Junior's house and barns and everything in them the leaves fall off the tree. Junior's girl Trixie sweeps the leaves into a pile and they rot. That is all until the next year.

My aunt is entertaining the smiling man. That is her part-time job. When she is not redecorating or shopping with Dora she demonstrates food slicers in your home.

She will bring her plastic machine into your living room and set the whole business up on a card table. After everybody plays two or three made-up games she lets you in on the Convenience Secret of the Century. She will tell you how much it would run you in the store. If the smiling man has a wife he can expect my aunt and her machine in his living room sometime soon.

Then on she will go about sorrow and sin and how is Ellen ever going to make out? Pretty soon she catches onto the sound of what she is saying and she pulls one word out to meet the next and once every sentence or so she will clap.

I hope the wise woman thought to bring her child an extra set of clothes.

Dora has soaked the seat of this car. My daddy is not aware of this but I am so I slide closer to the window to put some space between this red suit and Dora. Old as me and wets herself once or twice a day. I know they expect this dress back dry. Dora's mama would stand beside Dora dripping and deny her big girl wet herself.

17

You are right, Aunt Nadine. I promise never to pee in your girl's pants again.

She talks still but at least I can breathe with my nose outside. I could not ride like this for very long.

Dora wants to know if the smiling man will stop and get her a snack. Her mama tells her to hush little one but I could shut her up for good.

4

We have to drive through colored town to get to the church. They do not do anything but fix dead people and preach their funerals in this church. My aunt is so glad to be out of colored town. She unlocks her car door because now she feels safe.

Oh and wouldn't she like to be inside one of these white houses peeling cucumbers in a snap! And she will tell you about how everybody got his money and especially about the doctors. All they do is cheat, gamble, and run around. All anybody expects of you is a good honest living and to love the Lord with all thy heart. The smiling man probably lives in one of these houses and needs to hear this.

I do see myself something in one of the yards I want. And if he'd stop I'd hop out, take it and toss it into the trunk. I ride by here every Saturday but I have never seen that fountain until now. I would love to have it. It would look good in my yard. I could stick the garden hose up that baby angel and watch the water fill up and spill over the edge.

But I did not come to town to steal out of somebody's yard.

When we get to the church there are more people there than I know.

There is no reason I have to look at her. It would just give me something else to think about.

But I see Starletta and she looks clean. I wish I could sit with her and her mama and daddy.

Starletta and her mama both eat dirt. My daddy slapped my face for eating dirt. Oh yes but I have seen Starletta sucking in her face drawing what she can from red clay. My daddy slapped my face and jerked my elbow round to my nose and he ran his finger across my gums feeling for grit. She eats that mess like it is good to her. She sits at the end of the row while her mama chops. She loosens a piece and pops it in her jaw and squeezes. She sits and eats clay dirt and picks at her bug bites. Starletta has orange teeth and she will plait my hair if I ask her right.

I am in the family section looking out on the rest of the people. I do not know this preacher. He says that even though he did not know my mama he feels like he knew her well because he has met us and we are all so nice. It does not bother him that what he said does not make good sense.

And what else are you going to say when the Bible comes flat out and says killing yourself is flinging God's gift back into his face and He will not forgive you for it ever? The preacher leaves that out and goes straight to the green valleys and the streets of silver and gold.

My mama's mama is sitting down the pew from me and my daddy. She has already leaned forward, looked down here and called my daddy a bastard.

She has a tidy sum. Every Saturday one of her girls rides her to town to get her hair fixed. She shops and comes home with hats and dresses in boxes. When I go to her house she tells me to walk slow and do not slam the door. She acts like she doesn't know me enough to trust.

She looks like she could fly out of her chair and fly in a frenzy all over this funeral parlor. I figure by the end of the day somebody will have to pull her off of him. One year he showed up drunk for her Christmas turkey dinner and she took a running start and threw her whole self into his face. She is small and fast and wild but they say she is not crazy. Nobody would say much if she scratched my daddy's eyes out in private. But this is a public place and it agitates people when she starts in on him. Nobody wants to be the one that stops her. She calls him a nigger and trash so long and loud she gets hoarse. Just churning hate and nerve with forty years of my mama on fire under her. She may not sit through this service.

Starletta is lounging all over her mama. I know it kills her to stay for too long a time in one place. If her mama loosened up on her a little she would roll down the aisle and crawl out the window. In a minute Starletta will get her head thumped.

Amen and my mama's mama is up and out the door. She does not yell anything back. No nigger or trash. Just out.

And my daddy will fool himself into thinking that is all. She is gone. Good. I do not have to pay for her girl.

Close the cover. Close it down. Your mama has flown. She would not wait to see them close the cover down.

I will not look. No.

So why do I have to watch anymore? I saw all I wanted to see in the church.

It will rain before long. And we will come back to this grave in the rain and get some flowers.

Do not do that with everybody looking. Folks do not want to see a body disappear before their very eyes. Not me at least.

Do I have to watch?

21

Is she in there?

It is all done with lights said the magician.

Where is she? Not in the box. You cannot rest in a box.

Oh and now the rain outside and blowing inside this tent so people pull their collars up around their faces wanting to go on home.

I have found my mama's mama off to herself. Looking at all this through the rain. Like she has this funeral party staked out. Her hate flies through the rain and the wind to my daddy. He who has stopped everything but the breathing and must be brought back to feeling before she can hurt him.

It is done. You can look now. Some run to the cars but some come and put their hands on my knees. If there is anything you need please ask but no not now I will let you know. Somebody slipped me a dollar.

The smiling man pets my head and says he will take me home. His hand is big and warm and covers my whole head. I bet he will hold my hand and let me ride in the front seat. I walk close to him and smell his blue suit.

I do not have to worry about snakes anymore here. The pony scares them off and I am up high anyway so they cannot bite me.

When I stop to camp I put Dolphin nearby so he can keep them away. Then I do not have to worry.

The best way to camp all day here is to spread the pony blanket down and put your supplies on top of it. It takes so long to get from my house to the pine thicket that the pony gets hot and needs a long rest. I keep him tied on a long rope.

We can wait and eat. I forgot a book so there is nothing to do but lay back and watch the trees. They move back and forth like they know we would like a little nap.

5

When the smiling man let me and my daddy off in the yard I thanked him for the ride and went on inside. My daddy came in the house, got his keys, and left in the truck. He stayed gone until the next night and I cannot report all he did.

He missed some good food. Eating is the first thing I did after I got the suit off me. I folded it up and stuck it in a sack for Dora's mama. She had to get on home to take care of some things and would pick it up next week. I knew she would want it back. It looked clean and smelled pretty good to me.

Women from the church had made pies and salads. No meat though. Three jugs of sweet tea and a greasy bag of corn bread. I ate right out of the bowls and didn't use a plate.

It got late and dark outside. I made up my mind to go to school the next day.

Her mama died they will say.

I wore some of my mama's clothes to school. Nobody would know. Just some things up under my dress. She was not that much bigger than me.

I have a odd shape. But I am not ill formed. My head is too big for the rest of me. Just this side of a defect. When I get a chest and hips I will look weighted down. I have been waiting for them for some time now.

I enjoyed wearing my mama's clothes. Just so I am not in a wreck is all I thought. I went through all her things that night.

The stockings even the ones she had wore were bent at the knee and ankle and laid flat in the drawer. I decided to wear a little something every day. That worked out fine because the only thing I had left that fit good was socks.

I could tell the teachers were dying to ask me some questions. They had took up money from the homerooms for flowers. They did not have to do that so I thanked them. I went to the library over recess and my teacher followed me in. She wanted me to tell her how my mama died even though she already knew. She could tell her husband over supper about how I told her. When it came my turn to talk and tell all I marched myself right back out of the library room and out the doors.

I had liked the teacher. The only reasons for ever going to school had been to check out books and scratch her back during rest time. My fingers would smell like powder the rest of the day. She let me take up milk money because I know how to count change.

Starletta was on the school steps. She is not as smart as I am but she is more fun. That day she was rolling her socks down to pick herself. We decided to walk all the way home and not ride the bus.

When I got home it was already dark and he had the lights on. I went in and did not speak to him.

I did not speak to him or else I stayed outside most of the time. When they cut the lights off in the winter I had to ask him to take me to town with some money to cut them back on.

He stopped doing anything but drinking and sleeping. His two brothers Rudolph and Ellis came to the house and caught him laid out in the yard. They cussed him and put him in the bed but they came back the next day when he was sober.

You two are the businessmen he said to them. I never was much into business. You do what you feel like you need to. I ain't hardly able to take care of myself much less this farm, he said to them.

So they asked him to sign everything over and they rode to town to sign the papers.

Now, my daddy said when they brought him home and left him, now I can relax.

After that he was a free man he kept telling his colored buddies.

Each month one of his brothers would bring him some cash money in an envelope and I would make sure I got to it before my daddy did. They left it in the mailbox I guess because they did not think one of us was at home. I figured out what I needed and took it. You got the lights, gas to heat and cook, food, and extras. The people who sent the bills said do not send cash but at least I sent them the right change. I let him have the rest of the money and he would stock up so he would not have to worry.

I always walked in wide circles around him.

The only hard part was the food. The whole time I stayed with him he either ate at the Dinette in town or did without. I would not go to the restaurant with him because I did not want to be seen with him. That is all.

I fed myself OK. I tried to make what we had at school but I found the best deal was the plate froze with food already on it. A meat, two vegetables, and a dab of dessert.

Every week the school bus driver let me off at the store and I got a ride on home.

I hated to see it get cold. Starletta's daddy called the heat man for me and took me to town to get a coat. We went to the stores in colored town and he got me and Starletta corduroy coats. Mine was lined with sheep fur. Starletta said it would make her sweat so hers was plain.

The fish man kept coming to the house even though it got cold. He was a man named Jim and he drove a red station wagon with scales and fish in the back and boxes of candy bars in the front seat. I bought a fish regularly and he told me how to cook it. I bought a box of candy bars whenever my supply got low. It is best to buy in bulk.

I always had him cut the heads off the fish and clean them good for me. His fish came from the fresh water and I liked bass fish the most. I do not know how he caught the fish when the ponds froze over. I cannot feature Jim fishing Eskimo style.

It got too cold for me and Starletta to play outside in the ditches. That was too bad. Her nose ran all the time. Her mama started making her stay home after school.

I had to have something to do so mostly I played catalog. I picked out the little family first and then the house things and the clothes. Sleepwear, evening jackets for the man, pantsuits. I out-fitted everybody. The mom, the dad, the cute children. Next they got some camping equipment, a waffle iron, bedroom suits, and some toys. When they were set for the winter I shopped ahead for the spring. I had to use an old catalog but they had no way of knowing they were not in style. I also found the best values. The man worked in the factory and she was a receptionist. They liked to dress up after work. I myself liked the toddlers with the fat faces. Some of the children looked too eager.

Do I look like I am a leader of girls? When I got tired of the catalogs I joined the Girl Scouts. They put up membership drive signs at school and it looked OK to me.

There was some extra money in the envelope so I had Starletta's daddy drive me to town to buy my uniform and accessories. She yelled and went limp on the floor when I did not buy something for her. She could not have a uniform because they do not have a colored troop in my county. They might in town.

I suited myself completely. Canteen, socks, bow tie, Rule Book, everything official.

In six months I had all the badges except swimming. I wanted the badges more than I needed to be honest so I signed my daddy's initials saying I had made a handicraft or wrapped a ankle or whatever the badge called for.

I stayed in the Girl Scouts until Christmas. I got tired of going to the meetings.

Christmas came to my house with the people drinking egg nog and decking the halls on the television set. I am glad I did not believe in Santa Claus. As my daddy liked to say—wish in one hand and spit in the other and see which one gets full first.

Although I did not believe in Santa Claus I figured I had a little something coming to me. So on Christmas Eve I went with Starletta to the colored store and bought myself some things I had been dying for and paper to wrap them with.

I knew my mama's mama was having her usual big turkey dinner that night but that was OK because I had turkey sliced up with dressing along with two vegetables and a dab of dessert.

As long as there is a parade on the television.

I got Starletta and her mama and daddy a nice spoon rest. When they were not looking I had the sales lady wrap up the one I saw with the green chicken on it. Then I had the rest of the money for my own self.

It made my heart beat fast to shop. The store was all lit up with Christmas cheer and shoppers with armloads of presents.

I got two variety packs of construction paper, a plastic microscope complete with slides, a diary with a lock and key, an alarm
clock, and some shoes.

When I got home I wrapped the presents and wondered if I
ought to wrap something laying around the house for my daddy. I
did not have enough paper. He did not come home that night
anyway.

I wrapped them at the kitchen table and hid them.

When I found them the next day I was very surprised in the
spirit of Christmas.

6

You can see the smoke rising out of the chimney from the road. You know it is a warm fire where the smoke starts.

The house Starletta and her mama and daddy stay in always smells like fried meat but if you visit there a while you adjust.

Come on in the house is what her daddy says to me and takes my package. They pay grown men to do that in the more stylish places.

Her mama is at the stove boiling and frying telling the daddy not to let all the heat out through the door.

He sneaks up behind her and pinches her on the tail.

I saw that.

They would not carry on like that if they were at the store or working in the field. They walk up the road and pick cotton and do not speak like they know they go together. People say they do not try to be white.

As fond as I am of all three of them I do not think I could drink after them. I try to see what Starletta leaves on the lip of a bottle but I have never seen anything with the naked eye. If

29

something is that small it is bound to get into your system and do some damage.

They clean this house all the time but it is still dirty. They got dirt and little sticks all between the floorboards. They either need a rug to hide it or a thing to suck it all up. Her mama says you can sweep and sweep and sweep until you is blue in the face.

All three of them stay in one room. I myself could not stand it. They do their business outside and when it is cold they do it over in the corner in a pot. I guess they hide their eyes and hum while somebody goes. I hold myself until I get home.

And they never have had a television set.

The only one that can read is Starletta and she misses words.

Her mama works on quilts right much. She can do flowers, dutch boys and girls, just square blocks, anything you order. She sells them to white women from town and they turn around and sell them again for a pretty penny. That would gall me.

I do not know where Starletta and her mama and daddy came from. Maybe town. They live regular but most colored people have a grandmama or two and a couple dozen cousins in the same house. A family up the road had fifteen people in one house and when they ran out of plates they ate off records. Records like you play. I know that for a fact.

Starletta's daddy wears a green coat and a matching hat. Castro has a hat just like it. He, not Castro, has never bothered me and he is the only colored man that does not buy liquor from my daddy. I do not know what he spends his money on.

Come on and see what Santa Claus brought Starletta is what he says for me to do.

She looks at me and grins. She has one hand in a bucket of Lincoln logs and the other one headed for her nose.

She has a right to grin. Her toys look good. I would be proud my own self. A orange and green town that folds up in its own carry case, a colored baby big as a live one in a cradle, picture books, some socks and clothes, and the Lincoln logs.

Starletta still had on her nightgown and she needed to be washed.

You got to wash before I will play with you is what I told her.

She went and stood by the stove while her mama wiped her down and put her on a outfit.

I am too grown to enjoy most of Starletta's toys but if they are new I can make do. I know how long her toys last. Her baby dolls smell like her in a day or two and if she gets any crayons she breaks them just to hear them snap. I will not color with a broke crayon. I had her bring her last box to my house and I taped them back together like they are supposed to be. She did not like it.

We played and put the little block-headed people all about in the town. She does not go to town like I do so she had to be told where everything went. But even I had a couple people left over and had to look on the front of the carry case to see how they had it all set up. After I got it done I told her to get a hard look at it so next time she would know. She leaned in close and looked up one street and down the other but I knew it would not stick in her head.

Her daddy asked me if I want to stay and eat with them.

No. I'll just stick around until you finish if that would be OK with you.

You know you are welcome to stay. You know it's OK, her mama said to me. You know it is.

My mama

I stay and mess with the little town while they eat.

Do I have to watch?

I could go.

Starletta slides out of her chair and her mama says to take something you better eat.

31

Starletta is not big as a minute.

She came at me with a biscuit in her hand and held it to my face. No matter how good it looks to you it is still a colored biscuit.

Her mama and daddy get up from the table and one said they got something for me.

For me?

You have been a good girl. Right?

Lord yes. What is it? Is it in the box? What could it be in a box for me?

Open it up. Forget the hocus-pocus said the magician.

Open it up!

Oh my God it is a sweater. I like it so much. I do not tell a story when I say it does not look colored at all.

I think I would like to put it on now if that is OK I can slip it over my shirt and wear it I say and I think I need to cry a little.

You want to open your gift while I look or do you want to wait for me to leave?

That was mighty sweet of you. You didn't have to do it.

I had to.

Well well well, the mama says and gets up to put it on her stove.

I can see from here it does look good. It really brightens up the place.

I have to go now. I need to get on back home.

Stay here. What are you going to do when you get back?

Lord I stay busy.

You come on back when you want to, he says. Then he wants to know if my daddy is at home today.

I have not seen hide nor hair.

If he's there when you get home you come on back here if you want to. Come on back here, he says.

When I do get home he is still gone. I wonder if he has not drove off in the ditch somewhere and froze to death. Nobody would be out on Christmas to find him before he got blue and solid. If he is just hurt and gets froze can they thaw him out to normal?

Ask me what I would do in this case.

While he is gone I stay in the living room and watch the television. Whenever I hear him drive up the path I go to my room and stay until he leaves or I think of somewhere to go out the window.

It is much better if he is gone. If nothing jumps out at you to do then you walk around until something looks good.

I could dress in my mama's clothes but they are gone. A while back my mama's mama sent one of her girls here and she loaded up everything of my mama's in a big box and hauled it to the car herself. I just stood looking. Oh all the shoes and stockings worn and not worn. All the dresses and underthings and necklaces I never saw my mama in. She said to tell my daddy the message was plain and simple. Now get it right. It was she had rather some real niggers have my mama's things than any of us that drink and carry on like trash.

That is hard to figure out because you know I do not drink and I would not even eat in a colored house.

So I do not have the clothes to dress myself in. And I have run out of books.

The bookmobile does not run on the holiday so I cannot go down to the crossroads to meet it.

There is nothing in the world like that bookmobile. A bus from town full of stories to check out and take home. You take them back in two weeks and get some more. It costs to be late.

They get the books from the big library and it is like you are really there except you are in a bus.

Now I like that.

When I run out of borrowed stories I look through the ency-clopedias. I know they cost some money and I do not know how they got in this house. I do not even know if they are mine or exactly who they belong to.

The S book under sneeze has a picture of a man and his sneeze froze in mid air. They took the picture fast and the droplets number in the millions.

The P book has two poems and then they tell you what the poems mean. I do not understand why because they are written in English. They tell you all about poetry and list some poems you might look up on your own and enjoy.

Sometimes I read the Shakespeare poem slow and out loud with feeling because that is the way it sounds best. The one they have about flinging a scarve over the arc makes me want to whirl around and say it. Say it and whirl around and if I had my mama's scarve I would fling it and pull it over the arc and half over it and say it.

Dolphin and I have been in these woods too long. I have no idea how long we have been gone from home but it seems like a while. I thought this was a fine idea and it would have been if I had brought something to read.

We could go on back. You know they are all doing something in a group this afternoon. My new mama likes for us to do that every now and then but she does not push me.

There are five of us here. I like everybody but I do not know them good.

If Dolphin had a mind he would be glad to go back too. I put the blanket and the saddle back on him and tell him to go.

When we get back he gets a good rubbing with the wide brush. That is bound to feel good.

They are making a terrarium. She said last week she planned

34

to bring some springtime in this house. Who would have thought of this?

I can do this. Just let me get my coat off.

Oh yes. A terrarium. I have seen them in the stores. And we are going to make one.

Let Ellen put in some dirt.

OK. You have to keep the dirt off the sides of the glass so people can peek in and see how nice it all looks.

Have you done this before? My new mama wonders.

No. But it makes sense to do it like this.

That's good. Now let the others try. Everybody gets to put something in.

The last thing we all made was a fish tank. She got the tank, the fish and the accessories from town and told us all how to keep the fish living. Everybody was in charge of a fish. If they eat too much they will bust. Mine was blue and had lips bigger than the rest. I named him John but said I would change the name as soon as I thought of something extra ordinary.

Let me put in one more plant. A fern.

And that just about does it. Let's put it by the window so everyone can enjoy it.

The light hits it right and it will get some sunshine all afternoon. We all stand and look at it.

Are you OK? Ellen? Are you all right? Don't you like the terrarium? You did a nice job.

I'm fine. I'm just hungry is all I told her.

Well I would like to get your hair washed before I start supper. Go get yourself a towel and the soap and meet me at the kitchen sink.

It is the best when she washes my hair. Not that I could not do it myself but it has got so long that it is just easier for her to manage.

When it was warm she would sit with me on the back steps and comb out the knots for me. Where did you get this pretty hair? You have such pretty hair she would say to me.

I need a stool for my head to reach the water. She lets me feel the water with my hand and when it is perfect I tell her. I put my head into the water and it is warm over my whole body even on the places the water does not flow. She rubs and I feel her long fingers on my head and pray that it takes a long time for me to be clean.

Does that feel good?

Oh yes that feels very good.

I lay on my bed where the sun has come in the window and made it bright and warm. My hair hangs off the side so I do not leave a damp place.

I see the mirror from the bed. No matter how I turn my head when I look I still seem like a stranger in my own self.

My daddy showed up at my house less and less. I never put it together where he was staying. I do know he did not have the nerve to go out and take up with a hussy.

He did show up on New Year's Eve. Of course I went and hid when I heard him and a whole pack of colored men come in the door.

They came in my house and went through my refrigerator laughing at my froze food and fruit juices. They got my bread and jelly and made sandwiches and you could hear their jaws smacking all through the house.

I hope they choke. I hope they choke and die and I will set the house on fire and burn them all yes even my own daddy up and that will be all.

They call him Missa Bill.

Missa Bill. Ha.

I want them to leave because my window is froze shut.

Looking all in my cabinets. I hear them open and slam the doors looking for something to eat that is not froze.

Who said they could come in my house and have a free-for-all? Who said they could be here?

My daddy has got his guitar out now and thinks he can play like a star. He will hang his head and sing the Tennessee Waltz but his favorite is On Top of Old Smokey.

He says he will play a tune for old times sake.

Oh Lord they all know the words and how many are in there I cannot say but I know it must be five or six drinking whiskey out of my glasses and singing On Top of Old Smokey.

One tells my daddy this sure is a nice house. Shame for a man to live by his self.

My daddy says he has a girl running around loose somewhere.

That same colored man asked him how old is his girl.

He says I am nine or ten.

I married Delphi when she was thirteen, he tells my daddy. Yours is just about ripe. You gots to git em when they is still soff when you mashum. That is how that man said it.

My daddy did not say anything back but the colored men laughed anyway. I bet he made a face.

They stayed there for a while so I got in the closet.

What else do you do when your house is run over by colored men drinking whiskey and singing and your daddy is worse than them all put together?

You pray to God they forget about you and the sweet young things that are soff when you mashum and how good one feels when she is pressed up by you. You get out before one can wake up from being passed out on your floor. You get out before they start to dream about the honey pie and the sugar plums. Step over the sleeping arms and legs of dark men in shadows on your floor. You want to see a light so bad that it comes to guide you through the room and out the door where a man stops you and the light explodes into a sound that is your daddy's voice.

Get away from me he does not listen to me but touches his hands harder on me. That is not me. Oh no that was her name. Do not oh you do not say her name to me. That was her name. You know that now stop no not my name.

I am Ellen.

I am Ellen.

He pulls the evil back into his self and Lord I run. Run down the road to Starletta. Now to the smoke coming out of the chimney against the night sky I run.

Down the path in the darkness I gather my head and all that is spinning and flying out from me and wonder oh you just have to wonder what the world has come to.

7

I will give you a dollar is what I told Starletta's mama when she let me in the door. I do not care for the extras like food or the toilet. I know this is not a hotel.

She wanted to know what was wrong at my house.

That is funny to me.

I told her I got myself locked out just by accident and as soon as it is light I will head on back.

Her mama said I was welcome and to put my money up that they do not take money from children.

Since her husband was gone to look after his mama in the hospital I could sleep in the bed with her.

Starletta was rooted in good on her cot.

When I got up in the morning I was surprised because it did not feel like I had slept in a colored house. I cannot say I officially slept in the bed because I stayed in my coat on top of the covers.

I went on home and waited on the edge of the woods until I saw them all leave in the truck. I went in the house and then loaded up everything I damn well please in a box. All that was left to pay the bills and a bag of old nickels he kept hid where I had to crawl up to reach. I got two changes of clothes and put my Christmas presents in the box. It looked like the colored men had played with my microscope but they did not break it.

And what else do you take when you leave a place you never will come back to not even if you forget something very precious to you? You will just have to live without it.

Then there is personal hygiene. A toothbrush and a hair comb and towels in case you have to supply your own. To be sure they will have sheets for the bed.

Then there is where to go.

Get it right before you get on the telephone. You do not want to sound like a fool.

Hello. This is Ellen. I'm fine. I was wondering if

Hello. This is Ellen. I'm fine. How are you? I was wondering if I could come stay with you. Is this weekend OK? Do you think you could come and pick me up now?

I get lucky on the first try.

My mama's sister Betsy says sure you can come.

I tried her first because she has a recently dead husband and could use some company. I am sure.

It will be nice to have a girl around, she says.

That is sweet. Music to my ears.

You better pick me up at the store near my house. You know where that is? Our path is washed out.

And I am on my way.

What do you want to do this weekend? she asks me in the car.

Do you have a bathtub? I hope I picked somebody with a bathtub.

Why yes I do, she says.

I already know she has a nice house. It is yellow and has flowers growed all up on the mailbox if I am not confused.

I cannot think of what all I would like to do. This is all happening so fast.

She settles me in the house and we go shopping in town. It is a different town. She keeps saying she has always wanted a girl to buy for.

She did not have any babies. Not a one.

We shop and buy a dress that suits me fine and more little things than I can think of. My favorite was a pair of gloves with a sequin cat sewed across the hands. I cannot play in them but they are good to look at.

All afternoon and night and on into the next day is like magic. I do not think of anything but the flowers on the sheets and the bubbles in the bath water.

This is the life.

All day Sunday we just lounge around the house. Aunt Betsy spends right much time on the couch looking at magazines with stars in them. She just smiles and tells me to make myself right at home.

Which I do. Looking in the dresser drawers. Fingering the what-nots. Generally getting to know the place.

She just keeps saying for me to make myself right at home.

It is good to have somebody around like that.

Then she wants to know who is coming to take me back.

She must have forgot.

Take me back where? I wonder.

Home, she says.

I say I told you I wanted to come stay with you and you said fine. Now I am here and I got all my stuff that I brought from the other place back in the bedroom closet.

She says no and laughs at the same time. I meant you could stay for the weekend and then go back to your own home.

Really?

What did you think I meant?

That I could come stay with you.

Well I'm sorry for the misunderstanding.

Me too.

Good. Let's just take you back and you can come again another time.

My new mama grocery-shops every Saturday night. She tells one of the big girls to look after the baby boy and then she is off. I go with her sometimes just to get out of the house. If you get your coat and hat on and stand by the door you can usually go.

But if you go you better help.

She will not let more than three of us go at one time because that spells trouble. She took the baby one time and came home frustrated and touchy. It is hard to shop with somebody in the way. I took Starletta with me one time and found that out for my own self.

She goes at night to miss the crowd. That is good because you do not have people breathing down your neck for you to make your meat or fruit selection. It is also good because they slash the prices on the fancy baked goods.

I almost died when I saw all the froze food in this store. Way way more than in my old store. Here you could get every meal of the day froze on a plate. Breakfast. Lunch. Not just supper. Pancakes. Patty sausages. Link sausages. Hamburger meat already in the bun.

I tried to get my new mama to buy some of it but she said it was cheaper and better nutrition to make food from scratch.

But it is not easier.

She never runs out of money at the store. No matter how many bags she has she does not have to put a thing back to get next time. She pays the way I like. Cash on the barrel head.

Riding home in the car with all the food you feature how it will look and smell cooked. Chicken does not look like much raw but wait till you fry it. Then it melts in the mouth.

She promises to fry the chicken for Sunday lunch but only if I help.

Oh yes.

And please what about some sweet corn and potatoes or if you do not have any corn what about some peas? Does that sound good to you?

That sounds fine. But only if you help me.

Oh yes.

Aunt Betsy lets me off at the end of the path just like I ask and I walk the rest of the way to the house.

I will just have to lock myself up is what I thought. If I have to stay here I can lock myself up. Push the chair up to the door and keep something in there to hit with just in case.

I forgot sometimes and he got to me but I got him away from me pretty soon. If you push him down you have some time to run before he can get his ugly self up. He might grab and swat but that is all he can do if you are quick.

It would have been OK if he had left me alone to begin with but he got confused. Sometimes he would come stand outside my closet door just to tease me. Talking to me all about my mama's little ninnies.

You got girl ninnies he might say.

I became the champion of not breathing or blinking to be

43

heard. Somebody else calling out sugar blossom britches might sound sweet but it was nasty from him. He could make anything into trash.

The first day back at school my teacher noticed a bruise he put on my arm and they all had a field day over it in the school nurse's office. Calling in everybody but the janitor to come in and take a look at it. I had rather nobody saw my business.

The teacher said she was fascinated by me and my bruise and just had to hear more. She had been watching me close ever since I would not tell her about my mama.

She asked me how it all happened so I told her my daddy put the squeeze on me and that is how it happened. She was shocked but I told her I was used to it so do not get in a uproar over it. You live with something long enough and you get used to it. Like smelling the inside of Starletta's house.

She asked me if I had somewhere to spend the night.

Of course! I live in a house just like everybody!

No honey. Not your house. Let's call somebody to come pick you up and I'll take care of getting your things from your house.

That sounds good to me but I already tried it one time.

Who do you know to call? she wants to know.

All I can think of is Starletta and her mama and daddy but you have to call the store for somebody to give them the message.

Isn't Starletta your little colored friend?

You could tell by the way she said colored that this would not do.

She's it, I say.

I would feel foolish calling up Dora's mama or my mama's mama and I have already worn out my welcome at Aunt Betsy's.

The teacher says everything is OK and she will make the necessary arrangements.

That sounds good. Maybe she will have better luck than me is what I thought.

My art class teacher had been standing over to the side and not saying anything. I did not know her good but she liked the way I do art.

She got the teacher and the principal by the sleeve and said to have a word or two in the hall. When they came back in they said they had decided what to do with me.

It is about time I thought. Yes Lord it is about time.

8

I stayed at the art teacher's house until it got warm and green outside. The law said I could stay temporary until somebody decided what to do next.

She lived in a blue house with plants in the windows and hanging all in the kitchen.

Roy is her husband and he could clean a house like a woman. Wash the dishes. Do the clothes. Do it all and smile when you ask him how he can stand working like a woman.

She told me to call her Julia her real name when we were at home.

So many new things came at me so fast I did not know how to keep up. One thing we did was to go to a movie in town right in the middle of the day. It was a long cartoon and I cannot think of the name to save my life. It was OK to start with but it got long and I could not bear it anymore. They will not let you get up and mill around in where folks are trying to see the show so I went in the lobby for the popcorn lady to stare me down.

I put it all on the list to tell Starletta.

I slept in the guest room. She said I was free to decorate but it is no need when you know you will just pack up and go.

I kept my box of mess from the old house in the closet. The microscope came in handy when I had nothing to do. That was a good buy.

Word got out at school that I was staying with the art teacher. Some boy I do not know good had something cute to say about it. Just like me staying with Julia had something to do with her putting check plus wonderfuls on my art. Ha. He could shut his mouth or I would punch him is what I said. I got up close in his face and he did not say anything back. He better watch out for me is what else I said. I am strong as a ox.

Me and Julia and Roy laughed and carried on right much.

Every Sunday we would all three lay on the floor drawing each other with blue hair or two noses or something silly. You name it. Or we would all take a part reading Prince Valiant and stand up and strike a pose when it is your turn to read. That was the best.

The warmer it got the more we stayed in the yard.

She said it was good I loosened up. We would run around and she would tell me to let it all hang out. Let your hair down good golly Miss Molly let it all hang out. Go with the flow, she would say. Make up a tune and throw in some words and go with the flow.

I had no idea people could live like that.

If you did not know them you would call them off the rocker but they were just happy she said with a big H. You could see it leak out sometimes and she would grin and say don't you just love the sunshine or she and Roy would nibble on each other and speak some French. Sometimes she would grab me and say you are so NEAT!

One day I asked her what they were doing here and where they were from.

47

At first she said Pluto.

If I did not know so much about space I would have said OK and went right on with my business. But I said you are not from outer space. Where are you really from?

She said she would be straight with me.

Both Roy and I were raised in the northeast. We always liked the South so when we finished college we decided to settle down here and have a family

Me?

where I could teach and Roy could do his thing in peace.

Oh.

Our dream had always been to have a quiet place in the country far away from all the city hassles. Our minds were so polluted by city life that we needed all this space and serenity to find ourselves.

Oh.

She lived in the sixties. She used to be a flower child but now she is low key so she can hold a job.

She went on and said when she was young

Like me?

she wanted to save the world.

I asked her from what.

From people like your father is what she told me.

You mean there is more like him? You mean he is not the only one?

I need to know.

Once I got him in my head it was hard to shake him out. I mostly worried about what he might do about me making off with all the cash money.

When Julia said there was more like him I shuddered to think how God let him and the rest slip through. The day he made my daddy he was not thinking straight.

My daddy was a mistake for a person.

The times me and Julia and Roy worked in the garden I did not think about him but of my mama and the way she liked to work in the cool of the morning. She nursed all the plants and put even the weeds she pulled up in little piles along the rows. My job was to pick the piles up and dispose of them. I was small my own self and did not have the sense to tell between weeds and plants.

I just worked in the trail my mama left.

When the beans were grown ready to eat she would let me help pick. Weeds do not bear fruit. She would give me a example of a bean that is grown good to hold in one hand while I picked with the other. If I was not sure if a particular bean was at the right stage I could hold up my example of a bean to that bean in question and know. It took a long time to pick that way but you have that sort of time while she is humming.

I know I have made being in the garden with her into a regular event but she was really only well like that for one season.

You see if you tell yourself the same tale over and over again enough times then the tellings become separate stories and you will generally fool yourself into forgetting you only started with one solitary season out of your life.

That is how I do it.

Julia and Roy were determined not to use bug killer or fertilizer from town on their garden. They went organic. He mixed dirt and chickenshit and promised us tomatoes and peppers that would blow the mind. He would mix it all up with both arms up to the elbows and say how this was his dream.

I helped but only with a shovel. The hands were not made to dabble and scoop in chickenshit.

We went outside every day to see what if anything was growing yet. I made them bet me which thing would be grown first.

Then they told me one day my birthday was coming up so what

49

did I have in mind to do? That got my goat because I had forgot and could have turned eleven without my knowledge.

Do I have to decide now? is what I need to know.

No but do give us some time to plan. OK?

What do you think I should do? What would you do if you was me?

She wanted to know what I usually do.

I always turn the next age during the day then I go to bed and feel different.

How about a little celebration?

That is not for me. The only girl I know good to invite is Starletta and she by herself is not a party.

Sure she is!

She came to my house. Starletta came on Saturday morning and she brought the present and the little town just like I requested.

She was proud because she had only lost the post office and the fire marshal.

I took her right into my room and unfolded the town. I tried to trick her into letting me keep the town and she keep the present she brought. I figured it being wrapped up would appeal to her but she was not paying attention to me but to looking all under the bed and examining all that was not nailed down.

This was party enough for Starletta. She did not need cake or a matinee movie to have the fine time.

She liked the idea of scratchy carpet on the floor and all into the closet and under the bed she crawled on her stomach. She was in love with rubbing all her body parts on my floor.

When she got through touching in my room we loaded up and went to the movies. Julia dropped us off and said to be good and wait inside after it was over.

Starletta was the only colored girl at the movies and she was mine. When it got our turn to get tickets Starletta could not produce her dollar.

Oh God I said to Starletta and pulled her off the line where I could search her.

I told her to stand still and be lucky that I am not the police that will rough you up a little in the process. I searched all up in her shirt and around the rim of her drawers where a mama will usually pin a dollar.

I finally found the dollar rolled up and stuck down her sock.

She was better than I expected her to be in the movies. She squirmed a little at the start but when she got used to the dark and the music she went to sleep.

Roy had a cake on the kitchen table when we got home. It featured my name Ellen in curvy letters like a bakery but Roy swore he made it. It tasted the way you might expect pink to be.

They scared my pants off telling me to make a wish so loud. I wished I could make the wish later when I could think to myself.

Starletta stared at her slice until I told her it was food and to dig in. She did not understand how slices and modest servings go so I had to tell her when to quit eating.

Save some to take home with you is what I told her.

It made me grin to think of Starletta having some birthday cake after her supper. She took a hunk with the N part out of my name.

The cake left the table and here come the presents.

It was just Christmas and you know all the things I got then now just look at all the presents on this table. Julia said they went all out.

Starletta waved and pointed to the one she brought so I opened it first. It was not in a box but wrapped as is.

Her mama had made me a Dutch girl pillow to stick on my bed. You can always tell one by the hat and the shoes.

Tell your mama I thank her I said to her. Say it over in your head and out loud so it will not leave your head.

Roy and Julia gave me a round thing with colored pencils stood up in circles and circles until the white one at the top in the middle you use to make clouds with is the point by itself. You will always grab for that one first.

But the pencils were not all. There was oil paint.

We do not even have paint like this at school. I said Julia this is like your paint.

By God they are oil paints that do not wash out or off with water and to change a picture idea after you have started one you just have to tear the whole business up and start over. You can use them to paint something the way it is supposed to be not all watered down but strong.

I want to thank everybody for the party and gifts and Starletta especially for coming.

Old Starletta is amazed at all the pencils and little tubes spread out over the table. She would smear her whole self up like a trick or treat Indian if I let her.

I told her do not even think about it. I am serious about this art supply. You can have my old crayons if you need something to ruin.

When she was standing at the door for Roy to ride her home I gave her the crayons and her town. I did not ride to get her or to take her home because Roy and Julia were afraid of who I might see on the way. They lived miles from him but Starletta is a neighbor. I thought about him too and we all walked outside to say goodbye.

You tell your mama.

9

My daddy came my way. I did not go his.

He stayed in that house I know stewing thinking how to wring my neck.

He came to the school one day during naptime. We always put our heads on the desks to rest for a while. I cannot sleep in that position so I fake it. There is nothing to do but fill up your pencil tray with spit.

The day my daddy came to school nobody got a good nap.

My room then was on the front of the school that looks like a red shoebox. I heard a car sound outside and knew without thinking long that it had to be him. My whole self knew at the same time and my eyes had spots.

I dreaded to look at him. If I had seen this on television he might have looked funny but since it was me and real life I could not see the humor.

The teacher had to be on coffee break so I took over.

Everybody sit back down and stay quiet, I said loud. They all wanted to see what was outside.

He did not know exactly what room I was in so he made a general announcement for the whole building.

Get the hell out here is what he told me to do.

He had parked his truck in the flower bed the special handicapped children had planted. Later that day when they saw the mashed ground and the obvious dead marigolds they each threw little separate fits. The kind you would throw if somebody said the end of the world was coming up shortly.

He stepped out of the truck waving some cash money and telling Ellen dammit to come back he would pay for it.

Then my teacher came back in the room and looked at me like I invited him. She told the children to finish their naps but who would sleep when that man Ellen's daddy is outside?

You have to wonder what they will remember when they are big. A man coming to school? A man waving dollars and screaming? One man my daddy waving dollars, yelling and undoing his britches during naptime?

I told the teacher I could make him stop. Just give me a pistol and then go out there and scoop him up.

It does not even make me squint to see that in my head anymore.

I yelled for him to put his dollars on the ground and go back home. There was no sense in him leaving with the money.

When he heard me he stopped still like a bird dog when you blow the silent whistle. He wondered where my sound was coming from.

The police came in a while and slapped the bracelets on. We all watched him go away.

Somebody sent for Julia and she came to me finally. Her art room is in the back apart from the rest of the school so she had not seen the time but she pulled my head to her stomach and said to let's go home.

When we got home I stopped feeling dazey and wondered if he had left the money. She took the dollars out of her purse and then I had them.

Hot damn I thought.

It was back normal for a while until Julia and Roy came in my room for a chat. He did most of the talking. She mainly patted the bed beside her and held her fingertips up to her nose holes.

He told me the court believes you should be with your family now.

I do not believe it. It sounds crazy to me because the three of us could pass for a family on the street.

But it was true and the next week I went in front of the judge.

Julia bought me a dress for court we both hated. She said it is not exactly our style but there are some times when you have to play the game she learned the hard way.

It had a sailor neck collar and she said here is the worst part. Lace stockings and black patting leather shoes. Conformity she said.

When we went in the court I thought staying in the middle of Roy and Julia was best. My daddy was over there in the middle of two police but you still have to be careful.

And lo and behold my mama's mama.

I had not seen her since the graveyard and there she is again to watch this time.

They talked mainly above my head. Usually I can jump in and hang on to what you are saying but I felt so dazey in my head again that not a word made sense.

Then the judge in the box who was extra old to have a job talked right to me. He said he had grandchildren of his own and could certainly understand her point.

Whose point? I needed to know.

Then I caught on it was she my mama's mama. She was it. I knew when she looked down the row at me with the kind of eyes that say ha ha I got you now.

All the arrangements are made they said so why bring me in here and do this in front of everybody like Julia who wants to scream she says. What do you do when the judge talks about the family society's cornerstone but you know yours was never a Roman pillar but is and always has been crumbly old brick? I was in my seat frustrated like when my teacher makes a mistake on the chalkboard and it will not do any good to tell her because so quick she can erase it all and on to the next problem.

He had us all mixed up with a different group of folks.

On Sunday the food at my new mama's is as good as it can be.

The only thing is you have to go to church before you can have one bite.

Usually a child will make a fuss about going to church but we do not. You might expect us to tug at our hats and kick the pews but we know better. We behave like we are somebody because my new mama gets part of the collection money every week. That goes for our support, our food and clothes.

You go in that church and act genuine. Even if you think what he has to say that week is horse manure or even if you believe it is a lie you sit there and be still. Worse could happen than for you to sit for a hour. You could be where you came from.

I mostly read the stain glass windows and wonder all about who they are in memory of.

We have windows like the Pope has but his are art. I know all about that.

The preacher says that today yes even on this very day his word will free us from the torments and distractions of the mind.

It is hard to be a hypocrite. I look at the preacher and at my new mama and fix my face to look like hers. We all sit lined up with faces like hers. She says to be appropriate.

It is hard too when you want to smile at the collection plates set up on the altar spilling over with folding money. Every Sunday she gets her fair share. Reach down and give! I want to announce to the sinners.

All of us but the baby boy Roger is expected to be here on Sunday. Some teenage women tend to him in the nursery. He is much like Starletta except he is white and a baby boy.

We always get in here and to our places before the organ prelude. That way folks can see us and rest sure that their money is well spent.

Dora and her mama attend this church on special holidays like the Lord's Supper and Thanksgiving. They both glide all down the row and wish they had mink stoles to flag in our faces. They stay too dressed.

When I had to live with them a while we would come to this church even before I learned the name of my new mama. Of all the ladies in the church that could make into a new mama she of all people was the one for me. Even when I got back to Dora's house I thought about her and all that she looked like to me.

I watched her in the churchyard when she would walk straight and square down the steps like she might be a Queen or a lady going to be executed with dignity. Down the steps she would go by the gossipy ladies quiet and I always tried to catch her eyes. Lord eyes that would flush all the ugly out of your system and leave in you too much air to breathe.

She certainly was a oddity and I had to step back when I saw her and was not looking for anything in particular but knew her time was what all that I needed to grab. I would think when I went to the house and write down ways and tricks of how to have her.

Now it is done. It worked and I pat myself on the back each

Sunday I walk down the steps close as I can be up next to her.

When or if you come to my house now after church you will smell all the things that have been simmering on low. It has been waiting for me and me for it.

If I am very hungry my dress comes off of me in a heartbeat. Sometimes I hurry too fast and I forget to unzip my back. It is helpless to smell lunch through a dress that is hung on your face. I have busted a zipper and ripped two neck collars trying to strip and my new mama told me some things about patience.

I stay starved though.

Everything we do almost on Sundays has to do with food. When we finish the meal on hand it is time to prepare chicken salad, ham salad, bread, three bean soup, or what have you for that week's lunch boxes. That way my new mama says she has a head start and will not need to go crazy in the morning times when there is already breakfast to get in you and coats to get on you.

I know that ten years from now I will be a member of the food industry. Or I might read or do art. I have seen many pictures drawed or painted of food. They always appeal to me.

Everybody like me, Stella, Francis, my new mama, Jo Jo, but not the baby are involved in this Sunday cooking. Only Stella and me came with useful experience so we get to work the stove. My new mama says I fry a mean egg.

Today it is bread and soup. It does not sound like much but it is hardy and I like to show it off in the lunchroom when all the other people have a measly tray of this or that.

When we are in the kitchen we are a regular factory. It is just on Sundays we all get to cook supervised. The rest of the week we learn one at a time.

Jo Jo gets time off from the kitchen to practice dancing to her records. Not rock and roll but slow and no singing music. Some of the records I cannot tell apart but some of them I get in my head and use them for background music for my old stories.

I myself am dying to put on the froufrou skirt and slick top Jo Jo dances around in. Not for somebody to see me but to stand in the hall mirror and observe myself private and practice my style of posing.

She has been taking lessons at the lady's school all year and does she evermore love it. You can see her dancing even when she is only in one place or eating supper.

I myself can dance like I already said but not like Jo Jo. I had rather shake a leg.

My new mama says for me to wash the flour off my arms and do my homework. If you are like me you will put it off until the last minute and then Wild Kingdom comes on but that is just too bad.

I have a donated desk and chair in my room.

If the door is not shut good the baby Roger will crawl in here by mistake. That low it is hard to tell where you are at.

If I do not feel like company I turn him back toward the door and motion for him to leave. If he stays he is always hot to find something of mine to break or gnaw on. I keep my old microscope and art supply out of reach.

I usually hand him my gloves because they will not fit down his throat.

When it dawns on him to leave on his own will he heads off for another room. He has a mama here but he did not get a daddy.

10

When it turned summer I went to my mama's mama's house. All that summer was a bad time and no matter how hard I try I still remember her sad.

I told Roy and Julia I had rather go to the reform school or even get on the chain gang than go stay with her. I did not know her good but she caused a knot in me just thinking about her face.

They said they sympathized but there was not a thing they could do anymore. They said they would see me on visits which we did not have because Julia got fired and they had to move away.

She sends me a letter now when you least expect it.

It makes me slow down and sad to think about my mama's mama's house. All the time was like a record you play on the wrong speed.

Before I left I packed all of my things that would fit in one box and willed the rest to Julia and Roy. Some of these things might come in handy I said to them.

Maybe it is wasteful to scatter your worldly goods from hither to yon but I never wanted to have more than would tie up or tape down in the box. All I really cared about accumulating was money. I saved a bundle.

My mama's mama picked me up in her long car that was like the undertaking car only hers was cream. I told Roy and Julia one more time I did not need to go.

If we have to live together the least you could do is talk to me like you know I am in your car is what I thought to say to her. I figured she would warm up to me.

But all she asked on the way to her house was when does school start again?

Lord it just ended and I sure am looking forward to the summer at your house I said for the icebreaker.

I asked you when school starts. I do not need the commentary is what she said back to me hot.

So September. I said September.

I said my answer quick and on time like the army way. I saluted in my head.

I just kept guessing she was nervous around strangers and she would soften up. But if I knew then all I know about her now I would have jumped out of her car moving and high-tailed it.

For a while I figured she might have liked the idea of having a girl around the house but when she saw my actual self and my box she changed her mind.

You cannot blame her. I am not exactly a vision. But Lord I have good intentions that count.

I decided I would make the best of the situation because you can generally adjust to somebody with money to burn. She might be a witch but she has the dough is what I decided to tell myself.

But by July I called her the damn witch to myself and all the money she had did not matter anymore. That is something when you consider how greedy I am.

The first few days at her house I mainly walked around and looked but did not touch.

God she had it all.

A colored woman just to cook and another one to make up your bed and dust the what-nots. Not dime store what-nots you could tell but costly items. Collectibles I know now to call them. Egyptian type candy jars. She could sell museum tickets I thought. All this stuff collecting dust could go to good use. She could turn a profit I thought.

Her furniture was chiseled out of wood and the chairs had curvy figures on them not just brown or worn out. The colored lady said the pieces had aged and appreciated. And she said it like it was all part hers. Ha I said to myself and looked some more.

The curtains were not sheets sewed either. You could wrap yourself up in one and stay warm.

My mama sewed sheets for my old house. I always figured that was using your head.

My room was my mama's room she had when she was little. It had a canopy bed and a fireplace for show. My mama's mama said she gave me that bedroom because I deserved it. It took me a while to figure out that the room was not a prize or a present for being sweet. I started to think she knew what all I would see dancing around in that fireplace and how I would need the lights on all night.

She would catch me snooping around sometimes and say to me I'll break your little hand if you touch that vase! Not joking but serious to make me think of how a broke hand might feel.

I would go off by myself and imagine turning my buddy Starletta loose in here. She could have a rampage in one room and out the other.

Or maybe I will invite the whole family that eats off records. Nobody needs four sets of dish plates anyway. They can visit while you are at the beauty parlor I thought and I felt better to imagine it all. At least it was funny to me.

And all the time I was dying to know why she was so mean.

Some days I felt like it was a torture chamber and I counted the days until school.

I was there for a week when she said she had found something to do with me.

Finally I thought.

On the first Monday in June she woke me up with the sun and said it is time to get to work.

She has found a job for me I thought. I figured we were going out to deliver the newspapers. She would drive and I could pitch the papers out the car window. But she drove me instead to the cotton field and said to come home for lunch. Ask a nigger what to do is what she said before she drove off.

Five or six people were already chopping and they were way far down the rows and not noticing me.

I just looked.

Then the biggest lady yelled you better get on a row!

And I'll be damned if I'll do it I said to myself.

You better get on a row! she yelled again. The bosslady left you here to work not to stand. And I needs to make sure you do it. Now get you a hoe. When I gets to the end of mines I'll catch you up to the rest of us.

That was the first thing I had heard reasonable so I started chopping my row.

I lived on a farm with my mama and daddy but they hired colored people to do my part of the slave labor. I was too small to work right. I used to play in the fields with Starletta and watch her mama and daddy chop but I never figured it would be me one day.

Lord how did they stand it so hot? I wondered.

The big lady helped me catch up to them and they all told me their names that sounded alike except for hers. Mavis.

All I could think to say after my name was did they know Starletta's mama and daddy?

They go to the same church!

We started chopping again and I did not feel sick until the afternoon. I had to sit down and every time I tried to stand up I just had to sit back down.

Mavis fanned me with her apron and I felt much cooler.

Then she said what the bosslady is up to is her business but it must be a mighty bad debt you is out here working off. They is no sense in a white chile working in this heat. I can hardly stands it my own hot self.

I'll feel better in a minute.

You sit here and rest some. And you is not wearing a hat on your head. What you think that sun won't fry your brain? Lord chile.

The next morning I got a straw hat out of the garden shed and wore it all day. I felt cooler all over and did not get sick anymore.

While I worked I mainly counted in my head or recited the poems I knew good to myself. You can keep time with the hoe chopping around a plant. It breaks up the day that way.

I tried not to think and work at the same time because that made me slow. If I did think though I wondered about Roy and Julia and how the chickenshit worked out. Then I would need to get back on the beat of my poem.

Whenever I fell behind Mavis would catch me up. She said they were born to chop and that is how they could work so fast and steady. She would say that and laugh but it was not funny to me.

One day when I had gotten to know her pretty good she asked me why my mama's mama sent me out to the fields and why I was not in Vacation Bible School or at least somewhere out of the sun.

I told her exactly what I was told. My mama's mama said I was under her feet and besides that she could not bear to look at my face day in and day out. Also she said I might learn a thing or two out there.

Which I did.

I bet she never counted on me learning everything old Mavis had to teach me. The hotter the summer got, the more Mavis loved to talk. And I loved to listen.

One day she said flat out you look just like your mama. Lord chile you got that same black hair all down your back.

Did you know my mama?

Yes chile! I was raised up beside her on this farm. I knowed her good as I know my own self. I never knowed anybody sweet like your mama. Smart as a whip too!

She was?

Lord yes she said and laughed at the same time.

Did her mama make her work too?

Lord no! She won't cut out for hot work. Her mama made the other ones work like dogs but not your mama. You don't plan to tell the bosslady I been telling you anything do you?

Oh no I said so maybe she would tell me more.

She told me enough that summer to let me know I was not the only one who thought my mama's mama was off the rocker.

She said the bosslady had always been peculiar but ever since my mama died she had acted touched.

I did not need to ask touched with what because I already knew.

But still it is hard to believe in your head what you feel in your heart about a person. Especially somebody you know good. I figured one day I would do some encyclopedia research and see if there is a name for what ailed my mama's mama. But that was like trying to look up a word you don't know how to spell. What would I look under? Meanness? Angry? Just crazy? Then I figured it was a little bit of everything. And anyway, my family never was the kind that would fit into a handy category.

By July I was like a boy. When I started out both my hands were a red blister but then I toughened up good.

I thought while I chopped from one field to the next how I could pass for colored now. Somebody riding by here in a car could not see my face and know I was white. But that is OK now I thought to myself of how it did not make much of a difference anymore.

If I just looked at my own arms and legs up to where my shorts and shirt started I said I could pass for colored now. I was tan from the sun but so dark I was just this side of colored. Under it all I was pinky white.

At the end of each day the colored workers went to their shack and I walked to my mama's mama's. On work days she left a plate of something for me on the stove. That might not sound social to you but it was perfect for me.

We ate right many miniature chickens or turkeys. I do not know the difference. But they were baked and not crunchy the way I most enjoy chicken. When we both ate at the same Sunday table we both picked at our little individual chickens or turkeys and did not talk. And still it was OK by me.

After supper each night it was not raining I walked up the colored path and spied on Mavis and her family.

It looked like slavery times with them all hanging out on the porch picking at each other. They fought strong as they played and laughed.

I looked regularly but they never saw me or at least they did not mention to me to stay away from their house. I wondered right much about them and the way they got along.

My mama's mama did not pay them doodly-squat. I saw the

amount she had written on the envelope she handed Mavis every Friday.

She did not pay me a cent except room and board. I kept figuring up how much I was worth by the hour.

But Mavis and her family showed up in the field every day when I was thinking of how I would save up my money and leave if I was old as them. I guess it never dawned on them just to pack up and leave.

While I was easedropping at the colored house I started a list of all that a family should have. Of course there is the mama and the daddy but if one has to be missing then it is OK if the one left can count for two. But not just anybody can count for more than his or her self.

While I watched Mavis and her family I thought I would bust open if I did not get one of them for my own self soon. Back then I had not figured out how to go about getting one but I had a feeling it could be got.

I only wanted one white and with a little more money. At least we can have running water is what I thought.

The whole time I stayed at my mama's mama's I thought about giving that judge a piece of my mind.

Look. You made a mess. Now clean it up and put me on the right road is what I would say to him.

One solution I figured was to sell off some household items. It is hard for somebody like myself to be surrounded by all that and not think about how much cash it could turn into. I could make a catalog of her merchandise and let folks pick them out a ashtray, some brandy snifters, or one of the many vases. Piece by piece her house would disappear and she would be unable to do a thing. But I would be on easy street.

I would keep her tied up in this particular plan.

You would think that when you get older you get weak but that was not true in her case. Meanness made her quick like a jungle animal.

I started to think she wanted me around as a substitute for my daddy. And each day I was not exactly him but just enough of his eyes or nose to tease her oh she boiled violent inside.

It must have been hard for her to keep in mind that I was a girl Ellen and not a man she wanted to be alive by her so she could kill but wanted him alive too so she could work her power on him.

And she had some power. Without saying one word she could make my bones shake and I would think of ghost houses and skeletons rattling all in the closets.

Her power was the sucking kind that takes your good sense and leaves you limp like a old zombie.

That is how I felt some days. Like a old monster zombie who was a girl a while back.

But I got my fire back in me now.

She would take all the feeling she needed from somebody and then stir it up with some money and turn the recipe back on you. The money made it sweet and without it she might have been just another mean old lady. But set up in her big house she could make the devil scared of her.

She wanted me so hard to be like him. She reminded me all the time how me and him favored and acted alike. I never told her how Mavis said I looked just like my mama. Sometimes she talked so strong to me that I had to check in the mirror to see if I had changed into him without my knowing or feeling it. Maybe her wishing so hard had made it so I thought.

I decided I would jump off the bridge if I was different from my old self.

Maybe he did rub off on me. I still wonder sometimes if I am fine myself or if I have tricked myself into believing I am who I think I am.

So many folks thinking and wanting you to be somebody else will confuse you if you are not very careful.

It gives me nerves to worry about me.

My mama's mama would shake a little like this too. I hide my hands under my desk if it happens at school. It is not enough to notice good.

Her hands shook right much though when she told me about my daddy dying. But she managed to slap me with one.

She said your bastard of a daddy is dead and then she hit me in the face. That does not make sense but that is what she did.

I had not planned to cry over him when he died. I had practiced it all so many times that all I wondered was if he had died one of the ways I had planned. All varieties of accidents and unfortunate mishaps.

But he was somebody I knew who was dead. I felt the way you feel when they say a star or a old president is dead and you feel sorry for a flash when you remember his face and think about how you could go quick as a wink.

She was looking in my eyes for a reason to slap me again but I was determined not to give her one.

Go ahead and cry for your damn daddy she got in my face and said to me. Go ahead and cry. Just make sure you cry more than you did for your mama.

Why did she say that to me? I wondered and reached up to catch a tear I felt had just rolled over my eye ledge.

But she grabbed my shaking hand with her hand shaking and said to let that be the last tear I ever shed.

I still wonder how long she meant that rule to last.

You can bet we did not go to his funeral. I know they had one because my daddy's brother Rudolph brought me the flag they had laid on his coffin. He got the flag because he was in the war.

I did not go to the funeral but I imagined how bad the preacher must have felt to put my daddy in the same ground with good people and babies born dead who get to be angels. And beside my mama.

They put her in a box too and him in a box oh shut the lid down hard on this one and nail it nail it with the strongest nails. Do all you can to keep it shut and him in it always. Time would make him meaner to me if he could get out and grab me again.

Go ahead and look said the magician.

I do not want to look.

It is all illusion. Look in the box and see what is there.

I do not want to see.

Go ahead said the magician. There is nothing to be afraid of. Everything has vanished! See. There is nothing in the box.

Where did it go? I need to know.

Oh I suppose they put him in the hole and everybody walked away without talking just like before and they will wish they were already home.

Rudolph came straight from the graveyard to my mama's mama's. She sent me to my room and told me to stay there until he left. Which I did not do but I stood in the hall and spied.

She had some secret business with him. He came to the house now and then and she always told me to leave. I knew that what I was not supposed to hear was most likely juicy so I always listened in.

What are you bringing that trash here for? she met him at the back door and asked.

He said in a hang dog way he thought Ellen should have it.

I watched her get stiff and then she spit on the flag he had folded up in a neat triangle and held to her like a present.

Then she said to him after all the money you have taken from

70

me you have the audacity to bring that bastard's business into my house. You should be shot.

Rudolph had the nerve I would not have and said he only took what she offered. All that was due him.

She called him a worm and a farm boy too big for his britches. And if you don't think I can ruin you too then just hide and watch me! You just remember whose name that dead bastard's farm is in and while you're at it take a drive to the courthouse and check the name on your own damn deed. Then come back here and tell me who is running this show.

Rudolph stood there like the farm boy too big for his britches that his teacher had just unbuckled and dropped around his ankles so the paddle could sting and snap his behind.

Then he turned and ran out the door.

He left the flag though.

That night I woke up from my sleep because I heard something outside and I looked out my window and saw her standing by a wood fire she had made herself poking what was left of some stripes farther into the flame.

I did not go back to sleep that night because I kept thinking over and over again about the encyclopedias. Oh the froze sneeze and the poems. I wanted to rub my hands on the pages again. The flag on fire did not matter but just those encyclopedias. They might not have ever been mine but I believed that much touching and looking had made them into mine.

That is what I thought to myself while she poked her flame.

I do not know why I thought she would be happy when my daddy died. She was the kind of woman you cannot even die to suit. She would swear you did it to spite her.

We all did things against her she said. She even fired the colored household help because she swore they were an infernal conspiracy and were stealing out from her nose.

And when they were gone it was just her and me. Me to look after her not the other way around like you might expect.

That did not surprise me because I had just about given up on what you expect. I just lived to see what would happen next.

At least taking care of her took me out of the fields.

When she got sick with the flu all she wanted to do was talk. That was about all she was able to do. I called the doctor who checked her over and told me to feed her particular foods which I sent Mavis's husband to the store after. She told the doctor to leave and never come back and on his way out the door he could unload all the silverware and jewelry he'd stole. He just chuckled like he thought she was joking with him. Ha.

Then she said I don't need no doctor with Ellen here to nurse me.

Which I did the best way I could.

She wanted to talk mostly about my daddy and most of what she said didn't make any sense. It was like listening to three different conversations at one time. She could ask questions and answer for all three folks.

But one day she got up on her elbows and said to me clear like she had come out of a long fever Ellen you helped him didn't you?

Why did she say that to me I thought Lord did I do the wrong thing? But he said she would just sleep and if that didn't make me quiet then the knife by his hand would. And yes it is easy to see him now in the fog of his not knowing she could be dead soon.

It is like when you are sick and you know all the things you ever ate or just wanted to eat are churning in you now and you will be sick to relieve yourself but the relief is a dream you let yourself believe because you know the churning is all there is to you.

Go ahead. Push it in said the magician. Push it in and turn it a few times just to see if it hurts. See? You didn't feel a thing.

And through all the churning and spinning I saw her face. A big clown smile looking down at me while she said to me you best take better care of me than you did of your mama.

11

I stayed off by myself and figured most everything out.

I may not have the story exactly straight but what I do not say or know to say is just not important enough anyway to change the main things that happened.

Knowing or thinking I knew all she did helped me get along at her house.

Now I know what they mean by stumbling around in the dark.

When I found out her story I figured I'd march myself right up to Hollywood and get a Sherlock Holmes job. It took some real figuring to piece it all together and mainly I had to keep myself from adding more to the story than actually happened.

That comes from reading too many old stories.

My mama's mama kept a tab on my daddy and me through Rudolph and Ellis.

Then Ellis died.

I do not know how he died but I want to say murder. I know that is made up just because the story would go a lot smoother if he was murdered with a piano wire by my mama's mama who had on a black hood.

But all that counts is that he died and Rudolph was left to keep up with how me and my daddy operated. He reported to my mama's mama everything he heard the old men say about us while they chewed their cud at the store. He reported what the wives said about us while they squeezed their loaf bread or hung out the Monday wash.

Yeah old Ellen runs up and down the road with her little nigger friend they might say.

Yeah old Ellen is always bothering so-and-so to give her a ride home from the grocery store.

There ain't no telling what goes on in that house when the sun goes down they must have said.

And Rudolph would hear a day's worth and trot back to my mama's mama's like a yard dog with a fresh sparrow dangling from his mouth. Then she would pat his head and hand him one envelope for us and one for him because he did such a good job.

I could not swear all that is true because it sounds so extra ordinary when I run it back through my head. But as odd as I think it sounds I feel in my bones like I am on the right track.

I do not know all about her going to the bank and getting the farm and how she got all the land from Rudolph but all that counts like I said before is that she did it. And then you can move on to why she did it.

It must have got her goat when old Ellen ran away from him. That was very good for me but bad for him because that is when she let go everything she had been holding back just because she did not have it in her to starve a girl.

The way she arranged it was she kept giving Rudolph the envelopes to drop in the mailbox but she put less and less money in them each week. Only a little money each time so all he could think to do with such a small amount was waste it fast.

He could have ruined his own self in time but she was tired of waiting for him to wither up.

He would waste that little bit of money so in the middle of the wasting he might forget his life had always been bad and was getting worse all the time.

I always figured that a little imagination to go along with the money would have stretched a dollar here and there. But he was fresh out of hope as he liked to say about the wishing and spitting in your hands to see which one fills up first.

He was weak as water I have heard more than one person say about him. And that is just what you do not need to be if you have dealings with my mama's mama. She would come rolling in a wave over you and leave you there on your behind choking on the thing you had intended to say. And she could keep coming with her flood and stand laughing at you struggling in the waves of your forgetting.

That is how she confused my daddy.

I maybe should be sad and pray over him when I picture him fighting long distance with her but I blame him for making his own self weak enough to be beat to death by a little old lady no matter how mean she is.

Men and daddies are not supposed to be like that. But if you pet and groom your strong heart long enough you will turn it into a damn lap dog heart. But on the outside you still try to show off how brave you are.

All she had to do was wait for Rudolph to drag up his last bird. But it was a flag instead.

God if I ever told Julia all of this she would say it blows my mind.

Which is exactly what happened to my daddy.

He had a vein or a head fuse explode so he died. It makes my own head hurt just to think about it.

Her flu got worse when it got cold outside. She'd sweat and then yell at me because she was freezing to death. I had trouble keeping up with her changing so much.

That syrup I had been feeding her ran out and she swore the medicine had been making her sick all along. You cannot reason with somebody like that.

I just did the best I could with what I had to work with.

I never let her get up and go to the toilet by herself. You let a old person do their business alone and next thing you know you have a broke hip on your hands. I never let her take a tub bath either. It is too easy to slip. I washed her off one limb at a time. Each day I could feel the meanness draining out of her body but her mind was still wound up tight as a tick.

She never complained about the care I gave her. Just about my eyes.

You got that bastard's eyes she would say to me when I washed off her face.

So I would shut them.

I cannot help my eyes is what I wanted to say to her. But I just said to myself I will look after this one good and I will not let a soul push me around this time.

But what if I let her die tonight? What would folks think about us here in this house together and her dead and me alive?

Lord it can happen because it has happened before. But she won't die while I'm in charge.

I will let her sleep but I'll wake her up if she starts to die. I hope she can give me some warning. That is what I should have done with the first one.

Go ahead and stir yourself awake. I might have woke you by accident but all the good sleeping I let you have should count for something. Go ahead and cough hard. You wake up now.

I want to ask you a question.

Like what?

Well I know why you hated my daddy but what about me? Why can't you see I am not like him?

All I know is when I look in your face I see that bastard and everything he did to my girl.

But I did not do anything I say back to her and wonder at the same time why I said that because we all know it is not what I did to her but what I did not do for her.

And her gate is flung open and there is nothing left but the hearing of all she has left to say to me.

Why you little bitch. You set up in that house like the world owed you a living. In cahoots with your damn daddy. I know all that went on. You laid up all in that house with your daddy's buddies. I'm surprised you don't have some little nigger baby hanging off your titty. But you left before I could get the both of you at one pop. You and your daddy let her take them pills or more than likely drove her to it. And then you left her to die. And then somebody comes to my house and tells me how they found you all laid up next to her like a little idiot. But hi ho I got you now. You might have run out before that bastard got what was coming to him but I swear you will never stop paying for your part.

All the people who said things about me were wrong I told her.

But it was no use just like when you are standing there with the smoking pistol you found beside the bleeding man and you try to tell the police you found him there and you have a good reputation and this is just a terrible accident.

So I decided to spend the rest of my life making up for it.

Whatever it was. Whatever I decided one day I actually did. One day if I ever sorted the good from the bad and the memories of what I wish was true.

You just remember you are mine now she said and she eased back down on her bed and slept.

And while she slept I read by the window or watched her bed until it was an ocean and the blankets were waves I had never seen except in my head. And I thought of how far I am from the water rolling but I am here with an old woman breathing at the same time with her.

I could wake her up and ask have you ever been to the ocean? but I already know the answer. She has not. You can tell.

It would humble you I whisper to her sleeping if you for one time stood by something stronger than yourself.

And while she sleeps I think this would be a perfect time for her to die.

I sit by the window and fan the curtains back and forth to keep some air moving on her. She sleeps better cool. I fan those curtains that are heavy and figured like a oil picture. They weigh I know more than my own skinny self I know much more than the sheets my mama sewed for curtains. She would hang them over the windows and look at them sad like she wished they were out of a book or these that do not let in much light.

My mama's mama sleeps most of the time. All she says clear for me to understand is you best take better care of me than you did of your mama. And each time she says that I promise loud I will so we might not hear the other one who says kill her.

But I did not kill her just like I did not kill my mama or my daddy.

She died in spite of me.

I tried to make her keep breathing and when she stopped I blew air in her like I should have. She did not live but at least I did not slip into a dream beside her. I just stood by the bed and looked at her dead with her face pleasant now to trick Jesus. I said to her the score is two to one now. I might have my mama's soul to worry over but you've got my daddy's and your own. The score is two to one but I win.

I stood over her hoping she was the last dead person I knew for a while.

12

Wake up! It's time to go to school! my new mama yells.

It is good to feel refreshed on Monday morning. Not like when you are in a job you hate. I sit up in my bed and flip the pillow over for the cool side. Sometimes I even say to myself this feels very good and I count up what I like about the way I am living now.

Number one is that I do not plan to leave here until I am old. If somebody does try to make me leave I will chain my arms and legs to the bedpost and throw a fit.

Number two and three is that I do not owe anybody any money and I can count on food to eat that I do not always have to fix or be guilty eating.

And the best one number four is my new mama saying good morning to me like she means it.

All that bothers me about Monday morning is school. Julia always said it took her a while to get back in the groove.

While I eat my breakfast I compare it to the one featured on the side of the cereal box and it all matches. Toast. Egg. Juice and milk. Cereal.

That much usually holds me until lunch.

Got your books everybody? she checks.

Got your lunches?

Remembering my lunchbox is automatic for me.

Every time we get ready to leave for school the baby Roger cries and reaches his arms out for Stella to take him.

You can go to school when you are a big boy is what my new mama tells him but it is not school he wants but Stella.

I'll be back in a little while. You be a good boy she tells him.

He still does not listen to Stella or my new mama and he rolls his little fists in his eyes and screams louder.

But he does not have an attention span and soon after we leave my new mama will rock him and read a bear or rabbit story to him and he will be still. I do not know that for a fact but if I was in his shoes that is what I would do.

His mama Stella is in the seventh grade and she is the youngest girl I have ever seen that had a baby. That amazes me.

She is the official mama but she does not do it around the clock. That is when my new mama comes in.

If you just saw Stella sitting in the back of the school bus teasing with the high school boys you would not know she was a mama. Last week she dyed her hair yellow like corn and my new mama took her to the beauty shop and paid them to make it black again.

My new mama says Stella tries her patience.

Stella sits in the back with those boys and I hear her giggle and say to them you better stop. Then she will giggle again. I always bet one is feeling up her shirt but I do not turn around to see for sure.

I wish I had eyes in the back of my head.

I sit in the front seat of the bus by myself because I think this is a ride to school not a circus. Stella looks already wore out when she gets off the bus at school.

Monday is always music day.

I cannot carry a tune so I do not sing out loud for somebody to laugh at me. I just move my lips to the words and try to look eager and in tune. There is enough people to sing so that my not singing does not make a drop in the bucket.

We always go to the auditorium to sing because that is where they keep the school piano. And we always march past Starletta's classroom. I wave to her and she sticks out her tongue at me.

Lord sometime I wish I still had Starletta. Last month she took her hair out of the plaits and I had to say Starletta is that really you? when I saw her at school. I figured she would always have the plaits but that is because I always thought she sould be little and fast forever.

She has hit the growth spurt they talked about in my health book and she is getting tall. She has been away from me so long now I feel like she grew behind my back and when I think about her now I want to press my hands to her to stop her from growing into a time she will not want to play.

She told me during lunchtime one day she has a crush on a boy and she pointed him out to me and he was a sassy old white boy. And she would not listen to me tell her she would have to pick out another boy to love.

She is very sweet on Tom the white boy. A boy is a boy to her and this is the one she decided on.

But I know Starletta is not a fool. Her body is growing fast and so is her thinking.

Nowadays you can count on her to have some things figured out for her own self. But I still know her good enough to tell what is running through her head.

It is no use to snag a colored boy she would think when the white ones are the ones that have the cars and the money to set you up in style. Why do I want to chop all day and make quilts all night? she would think. What can a colored boy bring me for a Valentine present but some cheap candy or some paper he cut out and glued into a heart? But that white boy Tom could tell his mama to pick up something nice in town and she would put it on her account.

That is the way Starletta was thinking.

I know Starletta is getting a itch way down deep and low where a colored boy cannot afford to reach to scratch.

I always think about her while I stand in the middle of the singing.

The songs match whatever season we are in. Turkey in the Straw. Ghosts. Oh Christmas Tree. Easter Lily Fair.

If there is not a special season going on we sing about America.

I mean they sing about America. I just move my lips and think about how sly I am.

We both keep lists of what we need to tell each other. We started when I moved to Julia's. My list is usually more exciting than hers but that is just because I can go to movies and the grocery store. Hers might just say my daddy is building a inside the house toilet. Or my mama has a boil on her neck.

I wonder how long she will be interested in keeping the list with me and something tells me inside that one of these days soon she will forget me.

So I have to make a big very big good time with her that she will not forget when she is riding in a car with her white boy or dancing at his party.

I know for a fact I would not ever forget her but you can never be sure about how somebody else thinks about you except if they beat it into your head. At least that is how I am worried about

Starletta who never has said much good or bad to me but before long I will have to know I am in her head like she is in mine. It is good to have a friend like her.

All the way home from school I wonder if my new mama would let Starletta come to my house and spend the night.

That is brave to think about because I am not sure if it has been done before.

That is something big Starletta would never forget and she would think back on me and how she stayed in the white house all night with Ellen.

I wonder to myself am I the same girl who would not drink after Starletta two years ago or eat a colored biscuit when I was starved?

It is the same girl but I am old now I know it is not the germs you cannot see that slide off her lips and on to a glass then to your white lips that will hurt you or turn you colored. What you had better worry about though is the people you know and trusted they would be like you because you were all made in the same batch. You need to look over your shoulder at the one who is in charge of holding you up and see if that is a knife he has in his hand. And it might not be a colored hand. But it is a knife.

If you let somebody tell you anything else you are a fool because what I have told you is right.

Sometimes I even think I was cut out to be colored and I got bleached and sent to the wrong bunch of folks.

When I stayed with my mama's mama I made a list of all that I wanted my family to be and I put down white and have running water.

Now it makes me ashamed to think I said that.

All I know now is that I want Starletta in my house and if she tells me to I will lick the glass she uses just to show that I love her and her being colored is just the way she is. That is all.

I know my new mama will let her come. She will say something on the order of your friend is my friend.

That might sound made up but she means it.

I open the door to my house and look around for somebody to squeeze. And she is there each day in the kitchen and that is something when you consider she does not have to be there but she is there so I can squeeze her and be glad.

That always tops off my days just right.

She squeezes me extra hard on Tuesday because she knows that is my tough day of the week. Every Tuesday I try to think of an exotic disease that will sound deadly enough to keep me out of school. That is the day when the man comes and asks me questions about the past.

I always dread him.

I walk behind him to the school nurse's office where he tells me to relax and let's chat. The nurse is not there to listen in because that is the day she goes out in the field to give migrant babies booster shots. One day though she got back early and we caught her outside the office with her ear to the door.

He always starts out the same with how important it is for me to relax and say what I feel.

I do not think I have a problem but he gets paid good money I am sure to find whatever ails me and cure it.

So how are you today? he always wants to know.

Fine I always say back nice and genuine as I can make it because if I tell him the truth like I had rather be digging a ditch than be here today he asks me why I am defensive.

And then he will not let go of a word but he has to bend and pull and stretch what I said into something he can see on paper and see how it has changed like a miracle into exactly what he wanted me to say.

Then he will smile all pleased at his self.

Then he can move on to some new business like why I am not a social being. That was what he said last month. I told him I was not social because I did not want to be but next year I might after I got my own business straight.

He was not pleased with my answer. Or at least that is what he said. But I think he liked it because it was not as friendly as it could be and that meant he had his job cut out for him.

If everybody was friendly and sweet he would not have a job. You look at it that way upside down and the world will start to make some good sense.

Ellen? he says to get my attention.

I always think on my own when I sit with him.

Yes?

I understand from your teacher that you've taken to signing your papers differently.

I wondered when somebody would catch it.

Well Ellen he says like he might be a little confused his own self we could understand if you were misspelling your name but you've been signing Foster as your last name this entire term. Did you realize that?

Of course I know my last name I tell him.

OK then tell me your name.

Ellen Foster.

But that is not your last name. Would you like to talk about it?

About what?

About why you are using that name. You see Ellen sometimes children such as yourself who have experienced such a high degree of trauma tend to have identity problems. Do you follow me?

OK go on.

And these children express these identity problems in several ways. What I am thinking of in particular is the child who has experienced what he or she feels to be an unbearable amount of pain, and this child might not want to be himself anymore. Are you with me so far?

I understand.

I told him the first day that if he had to talk to me then he could talk to me like I have some sense. Just so he doesn't get ahead of how fast I can think.

OK go on.

It is not uncommon for such a child to pretend he is somebody else. He doesn't necessarily have to know that other person. Just so he does not feel the pain anymore is all that matters.

OK go on.

I don't know who this Foster is but it really doesn't matter. What does matter is that you open up and talk to me. Get that pain out of Ellen and she won't have to be somebody else.

Lord I say to him. I hate to tell him he's wrong because you can tell it took him a long time to make up his ideas. And the worst part is I can see he believes them.

Go ahead Ellen. Tell me what you're thinking. It's OK.

That may not be the name God or my mama gave me but that is my name now. Ellen Foster. My old family wore the other name out and I figured I would take the name of my new family. That one is fresh. Foster. I told him all that.

I'm starting to see your point. Go ahead he told me.

Before I even met Stella or Jo Jo or the rest of them I heard they were the Foster family. Then I moved in the house and met everybody and figured it was OK to make my name like theirs. Something told me I might have to change it legal or at a church but I was hoping I could slide by the law and folks would think I came by the name natural after a while.

He laughed like I had said a joke.

After he explained it all to me I felt like a fool for a minute.

Then I asked him if I could keep using that name anyway or if I needed to pick out another one.

I just don't care for my old name I said to him. I sure could use another one. If I have to give up Foster then give me a while to think up a flashy one.

When he stopped laughing he said we were back to where we started.

But I thought we had everything figured out I said. Foster is not the right pick so I'll think up something else.

No Ellen. The problem is not in the name. The problem is WHY you feel you need another identity.

Not identity. Just a new name I wanted to write that big across the sky so he would understand and the picking into my head would stop.

You are the one who is mixed up about me I told him.

He wrote that down right fast and then said we would discuss it again next week.

I said I do not plan to discuss chickenshit with you and then I left.

He will not be seeing me again. I might be confused sometimes in my head but it is not something you need to talk about. Before you can talk you have to line it all up in order and I had rather just let it swirl around until I am too tired to think.

You just let the motion in your head wear you out. Never think about it. You just make a bigger mess that way.

13

I was too smart to let somebody find me living with a dead lady the second time around.

They list names of funeral homes in the yellow pages so I called one and said for them to come load her up and she did not need to stop at the hospital by the way. I picked the funeral home that advertised in fancy letters. We Specialize in Embalming. That sounded reasonable so they got our business.

Then I called my aunts Betsy and Nadine and broke the news about their dead mama. I know it is a ugly thing to say but I think they were put out by her dying so near the holiday season.

Betsy said well what do you think of that and so near Christmas?

I was dying my own self to tell her well Betsy why don't you see if the undertaking driver will stop and let you shop a minute on the way to the grave? but I just said I thought now was as good a time as any for her to go. At least she didn't die and lay up in the house like they say my daddy did. That seems unnecessary to me with all the people walking around that could find you dead and report you right away.

Nadine just said she would be over right away like I had just told her she had won a prize off the radio and she'd be over to claim it in three shakes.

And she was not kidding. Quick as a wink before I could finish taking care of my project here comes Aunt Nadine bustling in through the back door asking me where is her mother. I pointed to the bedroom where you would expect her to be.

If she had choked in the kitchen I would have toted or pulled her somehow to her bedroom. Does she think I would leave her mama propped up at the kitchen sink or stretched out by the stove? I wondered. Anybody with any decency would honor the dead and fix them up in their own bed. Especially after my experience.

You learn by your mistakes.

But I had this one fixed pretty as a picture. I did not want a soul to say I had not done my part even down to the decorations.

I found her Sunday hat she never wore and tilted it on her head the way a live woman might pop a hat on to ride to town in. Then the best part I will always be proud of was the nice frame I made all around her body. I put all the artificial flowers I could find from all those show jars around her end to end so she looked set off like a picture. A still life you might say.

I finished up about the time the undertaking men and her girls showed up.

The colored boys that loaded her up got a big kick out of my project but Nadine said I was sick to do such a thing.

But I feel fine I told her.

I stood in the door and watched the boys work. One asked me if I thought I ought to be in the room now and I said I wanted to watch this time.

Did you really fix her up like this? the other one wanted to know.

There was only two of us here and she is one and the other one is me I said for them to figure it out.

Well I ain't never seen nothing like this before he said.

Thanks I said. I worked hard and I was in a hurry to finish up before folks got here so I could show her off. She does look fancy.

It's a shame she has to leave I thought.

But they carried her off and I sat in the room and heard Nadine and Betsy now start a fight in the front of the house. They fought over which one knew she was sick and one accused the other of ignoring her and look what happened.

You two go ahead and fight over who did not take care of the other one's mama. You two pass the blame back and forth like butter at your tables and I will stay out of this circle and time of blaming because I am not guilty today. And even when she was so dead I could not help her anymore I made her like a present to Jesus so maybe he would take her. Take this one I got prettied up and mark it down by my name to balance against the one I held back from you before. But I do not trust this newly dead one and when you look at her face you in your wisdom and seeing will know that her smile is a trick for you. But please take her anyway. And be sure I get the credit for it and if you can please show me some way that you and me are even now. I do not think I want to go through this again. I know I told her she had her soul to worry over but I lied to her out of spite. I am the one who worries about souls and I do not want to now no Lord I just want to worry about my own self now and all the living I got to do. So you fix this little deal up for me and I will appreciate it. You just mark down how I tried this time and did not sleep to forget. This last one might already be standing at the gate. I do not know how long the trip takes. You might look at her and say old Ellen might have prettied her up but she still is too mean to be here. You might say that to yourself or to whoever puts the checks by the names. But Lord you have to remember how good the first one was and forgive her for leaving your world. My mama did not know what she was doing. She was too sad to think straight. We get like that down here. You just fix that up for me if you will. And I will wait for a sign one way or the other that will show me how I am supposed to live.

So that is how I prayed in my mama's mama's room where I sat close so long by the curtains that hung heavy and blocked the light of everything that happened outside.

Nadine came in the room and told me to pack up that I was going to her house to live with her and Dora.

So I put my things all in my box and felt my whole body moving slow now to the record that had been on the wrong speed but was winding down now I could tell by the changes I heard coming on. And I put my things in my box and hoped I would not spin again to hear the same sound with nothing changed but the voices of people telling me when to come and go. And as I laid out my clothes and folded them to leave I reminded Jesus that this is not the way a girl needs to be. I told him again to please settle up with me so I could be a pure girl again and somebody good could love me.

I went home with Nadine and felt lonesome on the way to her house to leave all the flower jars I fingered in secret and the colored path I walked down with the same fear I had when I took the lid off a figured jar to peek inside. And I never found cash or silver change stashed in the jars but every night when I went to bed I knew I had found a little something on that colored path that I could not name but I said to myself to mark down what you saw tonight because it might come in handy. You mark down how they laugh and how they tell the toddler babies, you better watch out fo them steps. They steep! Mark all that down and see if you can figure out what made you take that trip every night. Then when you are by yourself one day the list you kept might make some sense and then you will know that this is the list you would take to a store if they made such a store and say to the man behind the counter give me this and this and this. And he would hand you back a home.

So I went back with Nadine knowing this time this would not be home so I do not have to feel sad about being here in the middle of a place so far from the house at the end of the colored path.

I will treat this like a hotel I told myself. I will stay for a while until I find the next place maybe with God's help but more than likely without it.

It was winter then and I had all but quit going to school. I kept expecting the police to come after me but they never did. If I failed tests the days I did show up then they might have punished me but I never missed spelling words and the numbers I did wrong were careless errors.

I always thought I would have more fun going to a harder school.

The second day I was at Nadine and Dora's was my mama's mama's funeral. They just had a graveside service I suppose because it is a waste of money to rent out a big church room when you only expect three or four people.

And I did not go with them because I knew all that would happen and it was not anything I needed to see twice.

So Dora and Nadine dressed up alike and left me in the house alone. On the way out Dora said for me to keep away from her room.

Which I took as a invitation to ramble through and feel what all she kept hid in the back of the closet and the dresser drawers.

I should not even have to say all that I found. Dora does not have any secrets from me but she has the idea that there is more to her self than there really is. Dora keeping romance books in the back of her underwear drawer was not a surprise. And I was not exactly blowed over by the boy movie star pictures under her mattress.

But I bet her mama would be shocked and she would cry because Dora let her down. And if I was anywhere near she would finally decide that I planted all that nasty stuff there because I am jealous of Dora's good fortune.

That might happen while I am staying here and I have to gear up for that kind of situation because that is how these two folks operate. I decided the best thing to do is ignore them like I always have and keep to myself as much as possible.

I declared to stay in my room except to go to the bathroom, talk on the telephone if somebody called me, and go to school. I thought about taking my meals in my room but I did not like the picture of me eating off a tray slid to me like I was on death row. So I would eat at the table like normal.

I decided too that one of my mistakes had always been lack of planning. But not anymore. While they were at the graveyard I decided that if I quit wasting time I could be happy as anybody else in the future and right now with one year ending and a new one starting up I thought now was the time to get old Ellen squared away for a fresh start.

And that is what I did. That is why I think I am somebody now because I said by damn this is how it is going to be and before I knew it I had a new mama. And I looked her over plenty good too before I decided she was a keeper.

I stayed in the spare bedroom Nadine's old husband lived in. He did not die flat out but he had a stroke of something and wasted away in here. I feature Nadine hiring a colored woman to look after him and saying impatient to her don't tire me with the details just say FINE when I ask you how he's doing. Nadine would probably not need to hear the truth much less see it for herself.

That sums her up.

So you have Nadine and Dora making up lies with the way they carry on together like they are getting prettier every day and what does not come in a shiny package from town is not worth the trouble of opening.

But I could tell them some things about what else can come in a box oh not the shiny kind but the black one that fits down so cozy in a hole.

And that is the difference between me and them.

I bet Nadine says to her girl some nights oh your daddy is not dead sugar Dora. He's up in heaven strumming on a harp with the angels and he's looking down at how pretty you are smiling at us both right now.

Chickenshit is what I would say. She might as well have said sugar Dora your daddy isn't dead. Why he's just up at the North Pole working away on scooters and train sets like a good elf should. Why he's Santa's favorite helper!

But they get some comfort out of the made up stories. And if that helps them get along maybe I should not poke fun.

But it is hard for me not to see the humor.

I think they were pleased about my decision to keep to myself. If a girl was staying in my house that I did not want there I certainly would be pleased as punch if she announced one night at supper that you will only be seeing me at meal times unless we happen to pass each other on the way to the toilet.

Then it got my goat when I had to ask for somebody to help me get a new round of clothes. I was growing again.

Nadine took me to the store and I told her just to let me out with some money and I would get exactly what I had to have.

It would seem like logic for me to wear the clothes Dora did not like anymore but neither me or Dora wanted to do that anymore. When she slung such a nasty fit when Nadine suggested that idea

I figured I must have sent that red checked suit back to them with a stain. But it was fine for me not to wear Dora's throwbacks to school.

I have my own style of dressing.

The way to shop when you have a limit on money and you don't want to be bothered every morning picking out and matching up items in your wardrobe is to buy everything alike.

Before you leave for the store you check the back of your neck collar to see what size shirt, sweater, and dress you are. Then you reach back and roll the top of your drawers back and write down that size too. That will also be your britches size. Then you look on the inside of your right shoe. Generally there will be a chart in the shoe department where you can figure out about the socks. But you will probably need socks only every third trip or so. They stretch with your feet.

Then you go to the girls department and tell the lady you need the sizes bigger than the ones you have in your hand. You follow her to your racks and say for her to leave you alone now please.

Also if you wear bad looking clothes to shop in the lady will think you are a little thief. I get distracted trying to shop and look very honest at the same time.

And you pick out two of everything just alike except different colors. But get colors that go good together like green and yellow or navy and white. Not a orange or purple you will feel like a fool in.

I always take a long time to try it all on and make sure I feel right. Then I pay for it and make sure I got my receipt in case something falls apart. I even sent the warranty in on my microscope. I paid good money for it even if it was the junior model. They ought to build things to last.

When I get back to where I am living I lay all the clothes on the bed and admire how it all matches.

When Nadine took me shopping that day I bought the most beautiful dress I had ever seen. I mean that. I saw it in with the ordinary dresses and I said this is the dress for me.

And the price was right so I bought it and it is still hanging in my closet even though it comes up to my tail. I have growed right much since then.

It is a dress you catch somebody's eye with. It is like nothing you have ever seen especially when I put it on and gazed in the store mirror I said Lord I could fall in love with my own self.

It has a row of lace around your throat. Not too much. Just enough to set your face off pretty. And then the dress is green like pine trees down to the waist where it fans out in a navy blue skirt. The sash is reason alone for somebody to want that dress. Already hooked on to the dress with a bow you do not have to worry with. It is the kind of dress that decorates you in the front and the back both. Even when I am walking off I thought while I watched myself turning in that dress somebody could look at me and smile.

That dress was the first sign my luck was changing. Some other girl and her mama could have snatched it up before I got to the store but no it was there waiting for old Ellen.

I could pass for a princess in that dress I thought while I turned some more in the mirror.

And the next day was Sunday oh the day I went to church and figured that woman with all the girls lined up by her had to be the new mama for me. And while everybody else was praying I looked over at my new mama to be and then up to the Lord and thanked him for sending me that dress.

I said I look like I am worth something today and she will notice the dress first and then me inside it and say to herself I sure would like to have a little girl like her.

Right after the service I asked Dora what all I needed to know about the lady with the girls. Like who is she and do all the girls belong to her or are they nieces and friends of the family?

Dora whispered back to me like she might be talking about special handicapped children behind their backs. She said they are the Foster family and that lady would take in anything from orphans to stray cats. Or so her mama said.

That fit my description perfect and I started thinking hard about how to be her new girl.

My new mama says sure Starletta can come stay with us and why doesn't she just ride the schoolbus home with me on Friday?

Have you ever felt like you could cry because you know you just heard the most important thing anybody in the world could have spoke at that second? I do not care if the president had just declared war although that is something to think about. I do not care if a thousand doctors had just said congratulations sir you are the father of a bouncing baby something. All that mattered in my world at that second was my new mama and the sound of yes in my ears oh yes Starletta is welcome here.

I will bust before I get back to school to tell her to pack up her bags you are coming to my house this weekend and be sure to bring some of your little rubber bands because I will be asking you to plait my hair again.

It is OK if you don't own a suitcase. I use a box my own self. Just put your pajamas and personal hygiene in a bag or box and bring it to school on Friday. Be sure and come to my class when the bell rings and we will ride the bus home together.

And then the most important sight in the world like the sound of my new mama's yes she can come is Starletta's face looking up from her lunch plate and I see she wants to come to my house to check if I have some more scratchy carpet on the floor or just anything for her to touch all over again that is mine.

You come to my house and I'll give you anything you want I

thought about telling her but I did not talk then about giving and receiving. I did not want her to think I was bringing her there to give her things she needed. It was just Starletta the girl I was after and she could tote my bed and my checkerboard curtains back to her house if she felt like it. But it is just Starletta I want to squeeze so hard she will remember that every time somebody loves her good. And I want her just to enjoy herself and let me give her without the talking all she has coming her way. Lord I do owe her. And all I want in return is to wake up on Monday knowing the two of us are even.

Lord then we will all be straight.

Then I will not miss her so bad. We will be even friends and I will not need to prove a thing to her ever again. And she will remember me good when she is old enough to think and sort through her own past to see all the ways I slighted her oh not by selling her down a river or making her wash my clothes but by all the varieties of ways I felt God chose me over her.

And I will tell you it is hard and not one bit decent to keep on with that sort of thinking when you have seen all this world has to offer.

So if Starletta is coming on Friday that does not leave me long to get my room ready. My new mama says she will do whatever she can get around to doing between now and then.

Well I would like to dust and make sure the floor is real clean. Then I want to wash the windows so she can look out and see the view I got here. Then I want to get her a set of towels ready. Do you happen to have any with a S sewed on them? I need to know.

She laughs and says she doesn't but if it is that important to me she'll whip it up on the machine tonight and I can see if it passes my inspection tomorrow.

My new mama is always willing to help if it matters to you.

I thank her and then I figure I need a list of all what we can do over the weekend. You just do not invite a friend to stay over and twiddle your thumbs.

Friday after school she can get used to the place. Then we can eat supper. Then Saturday we can ride Dolphin and that afternoon we might go to town. Or the other way around. Then Sunday I don't know. I always think of something in a pinch. I can change these plans if I need to. Just so she has fun is all.

And I let the whole lunchroom know on Thursday that Starletta is coming to my house to spend the weekend. If you tell two or three girls your secret and say you'll just die if they tell a soul then usually by the end of lunch people will look at you like they got some dirt on you. So I spread my own rumor and halfway hope the talky girls would dress it up from one table of other talky girls to the next.

I just want everybody to know that old Ellen and Starletta got a ground breaking planned for this weekend.

And make especially sure you don't let Dora Nelson hear any of what I told you I said to the talky girls right before they went to work.

Now all I have to do is wait.

14

Staying at Nadine and Dora's house was not as bad as I thought it would be. I had plenty of time to myself. Which is something I always enjoy.

The only problem is that all that free time leaves your head open for thinking and before you know it your brain slips a idea in and you have to shoo it away like that baby Roger clawing around in my business.

So I try to keep my head pretty full at all times. But as soon as a spare room opens up in there here comes somebody like my daddy settling in thinking he might make his self right at home.

But I got my own ideas about what comes and goes through my head and I intend to think about what I please from now on. But I figure it will take a while to get that system down pat.

Whenever I came out to eat or do my business Dora or Nadine wanted to know what I did in my room. I should have said I was going over how grateful I am to have them in my life but I was afraid they might believe me. So I just said I was reading.

What are you reading?

Oh I'm just reading ahead for school. It starts up again in two weeks and I just figured I'd work ahead a little.

Well aren't you smart! Nadine says to me like she is honest to God pleased. That surprised me and I looked at Dora and waited for her to say but I'm really your smart girl right mother? And then I looked back at Nadine and waited for her to say some variety of sugar Dora you are the smartest little girl in the whole world. Now they are both happy again and I leave them smooching on each other.

Lord I say to myself and wonder if I could have turned out like that.

Mainly I looked in my old microscope to kill time.

It was in good shape even though I had carted it around in my box. I kept the slides rolled up in toilet paper cushions and then I laid them in their little individual cases.

Nobody knew about those slides. I did not want Dora breathing on them and I certainly did not want her mama asking me questions. Something that small needs to be kept private to yourself.

I only viewed the slides when everybody was asleep. Then I would pretend I was on the brink of a discovery and then here it is. After all these years of research and science I have found the mysterious euglena. I had looked at that slide a hundred times and I knew it was made in a factory in town but that is the way I enjoyed playing. I didn't see anything wrong with it just as long as I kept in mind that I was old Ellen not a laboratory doctor.

Euglena was just one of the slides but it was my favorite. Euglena. That always seems to make a nice name for a girl. I think it is something I might keep in mind if I ever get a girl baby.

Two other slides came with the microscope. Diatoms on one

and a paramecium on the other. They always amaze me how they got something that little onto a glass tray. That would be a job for you.

When I got tired of watching the slides I could always draw what I saw. I still have a whole bundle of drawed euglenas stuck under my bed. They are not normal pictures but they are still pictures of nature if you think about it.

I want to see something live moving under that microscope. You would really have to work fast to get something swimming out of the water and rush back here to gaze at it before it stops wiggling. I saw on the public television the tail of something whipping back and forth magnified up close. Lord I would love to see that for my own self. One day I plan to have a professional model. I could stay excited looking at live specimens day in and day out. I might put that on my job list.

Nadine wants to know what would I like for a Christmas present. She says she and Dora plan to get me a little something.

All I can think of to tell her is a bigger microscope but she does not know about this one. I just say you two don't worry about me and just take that money and get your own selves something nice. You already bought me these clothes I told her.

But she said it's Christmas and everybody in this house gets a present whether you want one or not.

Well in that case I told her I could use a handypack of white paper. Not the writing kind but the painting kind. I only got five sheets left.

Is that all? she asked me.

That is all I can think of now.

Dora is not here to ruin that for me and I am glad. Nadine might want to look out for me after all. Maybe she plans to get me some surprises and when I wake up on Christmas she will have all grades of things piled up for me maybe because she is starting to feel sorry for me or maybe deep down she likes me. But the reason does not matter. All that matters is this year will be different from last year for no matter how hard I try and fool myself out of the memory I know last year was not the way for a girl to have Christmas. And maybe Dora will get the spirit from her mama and they will both like me after all.

But you have to be careful with dreaming like that especially about people you do not know good.

There is nothing though like a house decorated up for the holiday. A live tree stuck over in the corner lit up flashy. Everybody wondering if it might snow. I even put some holly across the foot of my bed and admired how festive it all looks.

I say to myself old Ellen has not lost the holiday spirit.

What can I give Dora and Nadine? Lord knows I have a load of money saved but it would take every penny to buy something to suit them. And I need to hang on to that money for my own business.

If you do not spend money on Christmas the only thing left to do is make any presents you need to give. Since I have a talent in art I can make a picture fit for them to hang on a wall. And even if they hate it I can still be proud of giving something I approve of.

It has to be a picture of something friendly they would like. Maybe some cats or a covered bridge. I can do both. I learned how out of a library book.

They could use some art on the wall even if it is the copied kind. I do not think they would go for one of my experiment pictures or the one I call brooding ocean.

So they get some fuzzy cats. They do not take long to paint but if you do not know a thing about art it will look to you like it took me forever. Then I sign my name Ellen swirly at the edge of a paw.

It looks good but it is not something I would have in my own house. But just as long as they like it.

I do not think they even know I have that talent. Won't that be a surprise!

I would really like to paint them one of my brooding oceans but they would miss the point I am sure of how the ocean looks strong and beautiful and sad at the same time and that is really something if you think about it. They would not like the picture because it looks so evil when you first look at it. It is not something that would grow on them. Not like these cats hopping around teasing with a ball of yarn. I like that picture fine except once you look at it one time you have seen and felt everything you will ever see and feel about those cats.

But if Dora and Nadine want cats then that is what they will get. I think they will enjoy my picture. And I can draw cats a heap easier than brooding oceans.

What do you two do on Christmas? I ask Dora when she pokes her head in my room.

I was just coming to tell you supper's ready. I did not intend to report on what me and my mother always do alone.

And she sent the alone part out to me with some spit and twist to it.

Well I intend to be here and I intend to know what to expect because I need to know when to give you two my present.

Present? she says just like I thought she would. Then she comes on in my room, sits on my bed and tells me the highlights of all the Christmases she can remember and she looks up to the corner of the room and I know she was watching all her past presents of dolls and playhouses and mittens dancing on the wall.

Dora I say when I get tired of watching her little parade my own self I did not ask for a list I just need to know how you go about celebrating. Like do you make egg nog? Do you stand around and sing? Do you exchange presents at night or do I I mean you get everything all at once in the morning?

She tells me they usually sit around on Christmas Eve and feel excited then Santa Claus comes that night and you wake up the next morning and you can be surprised.

When she was telling me her voice was all rushy and I had to smile when I said to myself Dora let me tell you a thing or two. There is no Santa Claus. And you cannot always count on getting everything you want. You'll see. And when you wake up that day and Santa has not laid out everything you dreamed of or he might have missed your house completely then you have to be brave and if you come to me we can talk.

But I just say Dora suppose you don't get everything you ask for? What happens then?

But Dora says I always get everything on my list and plenty of surprises too!

But I just say Dora suppose just one time Santa couldn't find something or a elf broke a item loading it up in the sled? What would happen then?

But Dora says no no no that would never happen and she pranced out of my room.

And I stood there feeling wise that I knew what could be true and what all could happen even when you least expect it. One day somebody's going to teach that Dora a lesson and this will be a big Christmas for her because she will have to share with old Ellen.

Her mama all but said so.

All I asked for was the pack of paper but she looked at me like she was thinking of some surprises or just some small treats to go along with it. She could not believe that was my whole request and I bet she is racking her brain to come up with something else

107

for me. She's already said I am smart one time. And she was nice enough to ask me if I wanted anything in particular. Yes old Nadine has something up her sleeve.

I just hope my present for them is good enough.

And just so it does not get lost in the shuffle of paper and bows and all the packages under the tree I better present the picture to them on Christmas Eve. Then it will stand out. Then she will hang it on the wall right away and we will all get a warm spot looking at it.

So if you two would sit there on the couch and hide your eyes I have a little something I want to give you. Just let me go back in my room and I'll be right back. Don't open your eyes! I say to them.

And I leave them on the couch together probably with their hearts racing about what they might see when old Ellen returns and says OK you can look now!

So what do you think? I ask them because they have not spoke yet.

Why Ellen that is really nice Nadine says.

Dora wants to know if I traced the cats.

That makes me boil but since it is Christmas I say no Dora I painted it all my own self for you and your mama to hang in your living room or anywhere you see fit.

She says that again about the tracing and I double up on the niceness.

No Dora. I tell her I drew these kitties with you in mind.

Her mama says they look sweet and she'll hang the picture first thing tomorrow.

What's wrong with right now? I ask her.

Well it needs a frame honey. A picture as pretty as that calls for a nice frame she said.

I reminded her that the store would not be open tomorrow on account of Christmas but I already took care of all that.

She wants to know what I mean.

And then I fanned all the frames I had made out of colored paper across the floor and told them they could have the frame of their choice and then I would assemble the whole business right here tonight.

Dora asks her mama if she plans to put some old tacky paper frame on their wall and her mama says she should be nice to me because this is all so cute.

But it is not cute and it is not a game I want to say. I wanted to scoop the cats and the colored frames up and burn them and forget I had tried to appeal to somebody and look at them now making fun of me.

But I left it all there on the floor and walked away.

And on the way back to my room where I stayed all night and half listened for hoofs stomping and bells jingling I heard Nadine say Ellen has tried very hard to please us and you have hurt her feelings. Sugar listen to me. Even though we might think it might be silly or a bit cheap-looking for us we still need to act nice. OK? Now when Ellen comes back out of her room mother wants you to be friendly. Now let's put that picture up just like we think it's the prettiest thing we've ever seen. Then after she's gone and it's just you and me again, we'll take it down. OK?

I stood in the kitchen and heard all that and you can bet it burned me to a crisp. I felt my chest all the way up through my neck clear to my hair turn red. And I walked the rest of the way to my room where I stayed all night not able to sleep with my anger and my shame and the loudness of my wanting to hear some something landing on the roof.

And I never heard what I did not expect to hear but there was the lie of the morning voice that said wake up Ellen and come see what Santa Claus brought you!

And I went in their living room and stood with them and the ghosts of last night's words and saw Dora already pulling the drawers off a doll oh just the one she had always wanted that walks and talks and pees like a live baby. And I wish I saw Starletta there again with her colored baby in the tiny bed. But it is Dora who has so much she does not know what to play with first and I still want to see Starletta with the town and the picture books, the clothes and socks and the Lincoln logs.

And all I wonder is why I do not hate Starletta.

And there is Dora again moving all around the tree touching all she has and stepping over the clothes and the socks to get at the toys.

So I will not get to tell Dora I told you so.

So she will not come running to me mad for the first time that she had to share one thing just one day out of her life. No she will not slow down in the circle she has made around the tree because there is no reason for her to hate me today.

But I have the hate in me strong when I wonder again why I have to watch this. Why does somebody bring me to see this that I do not want to see? I wonder and feel something in my hand that must be my present.

And Nadine says she knows that is exactly what I wanted and I'm so peculiar and hard to buy for that she thought she'd play it safe and get me exactly what I asked for.

And that was all.

So what do you do when that spinning starts and the motion carries the time wild by you and you cannot stop to see one thing to grab and stop yourself? You stand still the best you can and say strong and loud for the circle of spinning to stop so you can walk away from the noise. That is how I walked then.

That is how I walked then from Dora and her tree and Nadine and the pack of white paper I threw at her feet.

I stayed in my room by myself and thought about how much longer I intended to be in that house. I knew then where I was headed but I needed to collect all the particulars like the address.

Nadine knocked on my door a few times and said she thought it was very unladylike to throw a gift back at somebody. Then she said for me to come on out and we could all be friends.

That could make you madder than you were to begin with but it just depends on the way you see things.

After I had myself some time to be straightened out and not so hot I decided on some revenge. Sometimes that is the best thing but usually it just helps you to think about a revenge plan without carrying it out.

But Dora and Nadine would get the works I decided.

I could only think of one thing Dora did not have and most likely would not ever have and that was a boyfriend. She liked boys just fine and I even heard through a grape vine she promised a couple of boys she would let them feel of her. Then when she chickened out I imagine the boys were plenty hot. They say at school Dora is all flirt.

So if I could round me up a boyfriend and sport him around in front of Dora I could bring her down a notch or two and feel pretty good my own self. Except we are not in school over the Christmas holiday so there is nobody around for me to select as a appropriate boyfriend. He would need to be somebody smarter, nicer and certainly much better looking than anybody old Dora could ever scare up.

I still laugh when I think back on all this.

Since I did not have a boy to produce in the flesh then she just had to take my word for it. I had to be very convincing. And he needed to be somebody she would never run into and check my story.

When I had it all nailed down in my head OK I told Nadine and Dora they could come in my room that I was sorry about throwing the paper. I said everything they wanted to hear.

Then I said with all the excitement I forgot to show you something.

I did not say what it was right away because that would not be good for their suspense.

What are you talking about? Dora asks.

I had to make all this quick because I knew her head was over occupied with her own presents.

I said my boyfriend gave this to me last week when you two were in town. His mama rode him over here and he gave this to me last week and I've been waiting for just the right time to tell you about it. Lord I'm so proud I just couldn't hold out another day.

Well let's see it! Nadine says.

So I took my microscope out of the closet and said isn't it beautiful?

I had my toes crossed in my shoe hoping all this would work.

Dora just said ha! I didn't know you had a boyfriend.

Well I do!

I've never seen you with one at school. I can see everything you do at recess and lunchtime. I've never seen you talking to anybody hardly except that little nigger girl. I don't believe you.

Well it is true I told her hard.

OK then. What's his name?

Nick Adams is who I would have picked out to love if it was up to me so I said his name as honest as I could. I figured I was safe with him because of Dora's reading habits.

He doesn't go to our school. You're making him up!

Who ever said he went to our school? I asked her and made

my voice mysterious like Nick Adams just might be a international spy or a trapeze artist. You never know.

That really gave Dora and Nadine something to think about.

Then I knew I needed to draw attention off the boy and on to the lovely present he got me.

How do you like it? I asked Dora.

She had moved close in on her mama like I was about to bite her. Like she had just found out a dark secret of mine that I kept hid because it likes to hurt pretty girls with blonde curly hair.

How do you like it Dora? I ask her again.

Her mama says they have those things at the doctor's office and what do I think I'm doing with one whether a boy gave it to me or not?

I just say I use it to look at paramecia, diatoms, or euglenas.

Where are they? Nadine wants to know like I might be hoarding wanted criminals in my closet.

They're on these glass slides.

I handed one to Dora who reported she did not see a thing and who did I think I was to tell so many lies on Christmas?

I told Dora it took a trained eye and if she ever got enough sense to enroll in the smart science class she might learn what I was talking about.

And that did it for me. As you would say I was washed up.

Nadine said I was a ungrateful little bitch and I needed to have the hell beat out of me.

And then when she got up and walked toward me I told her flat out not to touch me or I would kill her. I said that low and strong as my daddy said it to me. I said it with my eyes evil so she would think about how I had been found in a house with two dead women and she might see herself just for one second as number three.

She just said for me to get out. To find my evil little self some hole to crawl in. That she didn't want me to begin with. That Betsy didn't want me either. That all she and Dora wanted to do was to live there alone and she would be damned if she would tolerate me or my little superior self another day.

That is when I told her I thought she was the crazy one. That she and Dora had told each other so many lies about the way the world worked that they believed them. You two are bumping around in this house lost and foolish over each other. You two are the same as the people who would not believe the world was round. That is exactly what you are like!

Then she wanted to know where I got such a smart mouth.

From your own mama is what I said.

Dora the whole time was sitting on my bed sniffling because somebody had spoiled her Santa Claus.

Nadine said she would call the damn judge at home and get me out of her house. She didn't care if I was eleven or thirty. She didn't have to put up with that sort of meanness from anybody!

So I packed that afternoon. I had not planned on leaving in a huff like that but when you have to go you just have to go. I had not even had time to do my research on where the Foster lady lived or her telephone number.

I said to Dora do you know that Foster lady's first name? I need to call her to tell her I'm on my way.

What Foster lady? she asked me.

The lady in church with all the girls. Hell Dora. If you kick me out of your house on Christmas Day the least you can do is answer a simple question.

Well I don't know her first name.

Well then where does she live? I say with my voice sniffly to match hers.

She lives in the red brick house between the nigger church and Porter's store.

That's way on the other side of school!

Well that's exactly where she lives. I don't make up stories she said to me proud.

Well wake your mama up and ask her the lady's first name.

No I will not. She's in there with a sick headache you caused and I will not bother her on account of you. But as soon as she feels better I know she is planning to get rid of you. And I'm glad.

Oh hush Dora.

I just kept packing my box.

Why are you so dressed up? she wanted to know.

Because I have to take care of some business and I need to look good.

Well if you ask me I'd tell you to take a bath and do something about your hair. But I don't care what you look like just as long as you leave.

Get on out of here and let me finish up. Then I'll be out of your hair for good.

You better wait until my mama wakes up.

You better hush Dora. I've done my share of that kind of waiting. You can wait until you are blue in the face but not Ellen.

And when I finished packing I walked out of their house and all the way to my new mama's. All the way past the school. On the other side of the store but just this side of the colored church.

And when I got there I ran a quick inspection and found myself fit to meet a new mama. She'll remember me and my dress.

15

I already knew everything I planned to say to my new mama.

Ever since I saw her at church I rehearsed what I would say and a variety of answers she might give me. I just hoped I had made a good impression when she spotted me at church. I had on the same clothes and my hair bangs were stuck down the best I could manage with just spit to work with. She's bound to recognize me I thought. I am not just a face in the crowd.

So I stood in front of her house with my box and tried not to think about where I would go if she said she had a house full of girls already. And I decided that if she turned me down I would just have to give up. I racked my head trying to think of another place but I was fresh out of folks. There was always Julia and Roy but I was too wore out to track them down.

I saw her girls moving around inside the house. They had the curtains pulled back and I could see her girls milling around. They will know of me from school I thought. To be sure they will remember me and say oh yes you're in the fifth grade.

I always saw her girls separate at school. I would have never put them together in this house.

Lord I thought that house could try out for a greeting card. Merry Christmas from the Fosters! it might say.

And I said then Ellen you can stand out here and freeze or you can knock on her door. So I went ahead and got my bag of money ready and I knocked.

I had saved a bundle just in case something like this ever came up and I needed some cash. I started with the eighty dollars I stole from my daddy plus the twenty dollars he left me at school. I picked up a little here and there. Roy and Julia gave me a allowance and I kept the change cleaned out of my mama's mama's pocketbook. Now I had accumulated one hundred and sixty six dollars to offer my new mama to be. That is not a fortune but you don't find many girls with that much cash to offer up front for room, board, and some attention. I figured it would let her know right away that I mean business.

She came to the door and there I was. I tried my best to look proud.

She asked me more questions right off than I could answer. Like are you cold? Are you hungry? Where did you come from? Would you like to come inside? What's your name? Why are you outside? Were you in an accident? Who are you?

Lord I said to myself she is really interested in me.

I started out by saying I would like to come in and no I have not been in a accident. I came here by myself. I mean to be here.

I went in her house that smelled like a Christmas tree and I saw fruit laying all around in bowls. And somebody fried a chicken in this house yesterday. I could smell that separate from the Christmas tree scent and I wondered if they had any wings or thighs left in the refrigerator.

Why don't you come back here and warm up? Come on back to my room she said to me and then she yelled for Stella to take my box for me. Stella and the other girls had the parades turned up loud and they were sprawled out on the floor relaxing like you are supposed to do on Christmas Day.

I followed her back to her room and took off my coat.

And she noticed my dress right away.

What a pretty dress! she said. You sure are mighty spiffed up to be out walking on Christmas. Tell me honey. Did you run away?

I told her I did not. I am not in trouble I said but I do need a place to stay. What do you think of me staying here?

Well I've had some pretty unusual requests before but this is the strangest yet. I need to find out who you are and a few other things like your parents' names. Are you sure you didn't run away from home? I bet your mom and dad are pretty worried about you right now.

No they aren't. They are both dead and I have just been thrown out of my aunt's house. You might know her. Nadine Nelson. But it is no use to call her and ask her to come fetch me back. She told me flat out to leave.

Well how did you know to come here?

Last Sunday at church I saw you and your girls and I asked Dora who you were. She told me and I figured since you already had some girls about my size that you might be able to squeeze me in. I planned to come on New Year's but here I am today.

I usually get children referred to me through the court. I've never had a situation like this. Let me think on this.

I can sleep on a cot.

Oh the room for you isn't a problem. I have a bedroom that's not in use. It's just more complicated than you know.

Well I got something to help you make up your mind.

What?

118

And I shook my cash money out on her bed and said it's one hundred and sixty six dollars there. You can count it yourself if you don't believe me. It's mostly in one dollars so it looks like it's more than that. But I want to pay you that money so we can keep this all on the up in up. That way you and me will be even. You get the money and I stay here until I graduate from high school. How does that sound to you?

I can't take this money. I tell you what. I'm going to call County Social Services first thing in the morning and we'll get the ball rolling. I can't promise you anything but if you need a place as badly as it appears then we would welcome you here.

That sounded a little bit like something from one of my old books but I had waited so long to believe somebody that I just listened and believed.

And then she hugged me. She leaned over me and pulled me up next to her and it was just like I wanted it to be.

That is when she squatted down in front of me and asked me my name. I told her Ellen then she said Ellen I bet you never thought old Santa Claus would bring you a new mama for Christmas.

That is where I got the name new mama.

And then she got teary eyed and I told her there was just a couple of things I needed to know before I unloaded my box and settled in that room she mentioned.

What's that?

Well I need to know if you are pretty healthy or if you have a disease or bad habits like drinking. Also are you generally friendly or do you have days when you act crazy or extra mean?

Why Ellen?

I just need to know.

OK. I'm healthy as a horse. Nobody here drinks or smokes. And to have a house full of children I think I'm pretty even tempered. How's that?

Thanks I said. That's exactly what I needed to know.

Great! Now let's get you settled in a room and then I'll get supper on the table. I bet you're starved.

I sure am. Do you happen to have some cold chicken in your refrigerator? I thought I smelled some on the way in.

That's quite a nose you have there she laughed and said at the same time. I haven't cooked chicken in three days!

Well something that good generally hangs in the air a while.

And while she fixed supper I unpacked my box and laid down to look out the window. I was glad to rest. My arms were sore from toting the box and even when I laid out flat and still my legs felt like they were walking again. But I would not move ever from there.

I have laid in my bed many many days since that first afternoon I heard her in the kitchen and I am always as glad to rest as I was then. That day I looked around the room at the curtains and bed spread and the pillow sacks the girl before me picked out. My new mama sewed for her too.

Sometimes I wonder what the girl is doing now and I bet to myself she is not a crook no I bet she is somebody decent because she had somebody decent to love her good. She might not have had all the money I had to pay her new mama but she got some dingleball curtains and clothes sewed for her anyway.

My new mama never spent my money. She keeps it pushed back in the hall closet. I found it one day when I was rambling. The money bag has my name Ellen on it and the date I moved in here.

Now I can turn out to be different too. I could have been a hobo. If my new mama and her girls had been gone on a vacation there is no telling where old Ellen might have turned up.

If I think about my life like that I can see how lucky I am.

Since my first day here all I felt is luck coming my way. I never thought I could have it this good. The other girls know they are lucky to be here too. Nobody ever says it out loud but whenever I hear Stella crying in her room and then I hear my new mama tell her she understands and she is a good girl not a bad girl then I know Stella is having her back rubbed and I know she is glad to feel her new mama's hands.

You don't need to see through the walls here to know when my new mama is alone with one of her girls telling them about how to be strong or rubbing their backs. You can imagine it easy if it has happened to you.

And there have been more than a plenty days when she has put both my hands in hers and said if we relax and breathe slow together I can slow down shaking. And it always works.

And there was a day last year when she said if I didn't cry sooner or later I would bust. That is something I am still working on. I think how good it would feel but there is always my mama's mama's voice telling me to cry so she can slap me. My new mama says all that will be over soon. She said that with a guarantee.

I have some other things to work on but at least I am somewhere friendly and nothing new bad has happened to me since I got here. That is something when you think about it.

Nobody has died or blamed me for anything worse than over-watering the terrarium. But you can always stick some more ferns in the dirt. My new mama said it was not the end of the world.

Every day I try to feel a little better about all that went on when I was little. About all I have big to straighten out is me and Starletta. But I can take care of that this weekend.

You know she will be here after school today. And I am ready.

My new mama sewed the S's on a set of towels just for Starletta. That would really be something to walk in a white toilet and there is a bathtub clean as a whistle and towels just for you.

I wonder if Starletta would let me take a bath with her. She might already be modest though. She has started to walk with a little twist since she unplaited her hair.

But I told her to bring her hair supplies. I sure would like to feel her fingers working fast in my hair again.

Her name is all I can think about and when I hand my breakfast dishes to my new mama I say you remember Starletta's coming home with me this afternoon right?

Yes and I think we're all ready for the big event she says and laughs a little.

Then when the bus comes I need to tell the driver first thing that I'll be having a extra passenger on board this afternoon. She'll be getting off at my house. She's colored but don't act like you notice. And she'll be sitting right up front with me. And she'll be getting off at my house.

He just says for me to hurry up and sit down and then he looks back at me in the rear view mirror like I am a nut.

I'm just all excited I want to say to him.

God a day can go by slow when you are dying for it to fly.

Oh Starletta I say in my head all morning and then I go in the lunchroom and see her mama has her scrubbed gleaming brown and Lord look at her all dressed up in a jumper and a round neck collar shirt. She has on her Sunday shoes. And I know without looking her drawers have rows and rows of lace across the tail.

It is all I can do not to break out of my lunch line and run over there and make sure she brought her suitcase or bag or box or just anything just as long as she didn't forget she's coming home with me today.

But I wait to buy my milk in the line like I should. Then I find her sitting with all her colored friends and I say loud have you got everything all packed to come to my house all weekend?

And she reaches under the table and drags up a grocery bag

folded over at the top I know is filled with pajamas and drawers and her personal hygiene.

Good.

Well you meet me at my classroom when the bell rings and I'll take you to my bus. OK?

And then I eat my soup and dread the afternoon and all that time that is keeping me and Starletta apart.

By the time the bell finally does ring I am so wore out with the waiting I say to myself I could use a nap before we start playing. But it is too late for that.

I do not say much on the bus. I figure I'll do all my talking when I have her to myself. Or maybe not so much talking. Just right much doing.

I have changed my plans for the weekend three times and I finally have something I can live with.

First we will get off the bus. Then we'll go inside and she can meet my new mama. I already told my new mama I would like for her to make a fuss over how pretty Starletta is. But not the kind of fuss that says you sure are pretty to be colored. The kind that says you sure are pretty and that is all. The other way does not count.

Then we'll put her belongings away in the drawer I have cleared out special. And then I'll direct her to the toilet and stand back while she sees the bathtub and her towels.

That is right much for somebody to take in all at one time so I thought then we would lay down and rest until supper. Then she could see how I enjoy staying laid up in my bed waiting for supper to cook.

And you can guess what all is on the menu.

And when my new mama greets Starletta she says everything perfect just like we rehearsed and like she means it her own self. It sounds so good to me because I know it is true.

So this is Starletta she says. Ellen told me what a pretty girl you are and I can see it is the truth. I want you to make yourself right at home this weekend and if there is anything you need you just let me know.

We had not rehearsed that last part. I think that is a nice touch.

Then my new mama squeezes all of her girls hello and I introduce Starletta to Roger. He does not want to meet anybody new right now because he is loving up on Stella.

OK everybody has met you so let's go on back here and I'll show you where to put your stuff.

Starletta looks all around at how clean everything is and I know she has her eye on the scratchy carpet so I tell her my new mama sucks all the dirt up with a thing and you could roll all over this house and never get dirty. I can look in her eyes and see her mark that down on her list of things to do this weekend.

When she puts her clothes away and after I show her the toilet I say we need to rest a while because that is what I always do between school and supper.

But what I really want to do is get her off by herself so I can talk to her good. I need to tell her about what all I have up my sleeve fun for the weekend and then I have some big things to tell her.

You change out of your school clothes and put on some britches. Did you bring some britches? If you didn't you can probably fit into a pair of mine. You are about as big as me. Look at us there in the mirror.

She is still about a hand smaller than me though.

Come on and crawl up here and rest with me for a while. This is the way I always do.

Let's talk some now. I'll start I say to her but I do not look at her face but up at the ceiling but I feel her laid flat and still beside me waiting for me to begin.

Starletta I've looked forward to you coming to my house and I hope you have a fine time here. I sure like it here. Do you remember me living with my daddy and how I used to come to your house so much?

I sure do she says to me and it takes twice as long for her to get that out as normal because she stutters bad and she gets frustrated.

Well I came to your house so much because I did not want to be with my daddy and mostly because I like you so much. Even if my daddy had been the president I would have still run down to your house whenever I needed to play. Do you believe me?

And I look at her so she can nod and will not need to speak. She hates to talk.

Starletta I always thought I was special because I was white and when I thought about you being colored I said to myself it sure is a shame Starletta's colored. I sure would hate to be that way. White people selling your mama's quilts like they do. And the three of you live in that house that's about to fall down. I always went away from your house wondering how you stood to live without a inside toilet. I know your daddy just put one in but you went a long time without one. Longer than any white folks I know. And when I thought about you I always felt glad for myself. And now I don't know why. I really don't. And I just wanted to tell you that. You don't have to say anything back. You just lay there and wait for supper.

And I will lay here too and wait for supper beside a girl that every rule in the book says I should not have in my house much less laid still and sleeping by me.

But while I watch her asleep now I remember that they changed that rule. So it does not make any sense for me to feel like I'm breaking the law.

Nobody but a handful of folks I know pays attention to rules about how you treat somebody anyway. But as I lay in that bed and watch my Starletta fall asleep I figure that if they could fight a war over how I'm supposed to think about her then I'm obligated to do it. It seems like the decent thing to do.

I came a long way to get here but when you think about it real hard you will see that old Starletta came even farther.

And I watch her resting now because soon we'll all be eating supper and maybe some cake tonight and I say low Starletta you sure have a right to rest.

And all this time I thought I had the hardest row to hoe.

That will always amaze me.

About the Author

Kaye Gibbons was born in rural Nash County, North Carolina, in 1960. She attended North Carolina State University and the University of North Carolina at Chapel Hill. Her second novel, *A Virtuous Woman*, will be published by Algonquin Books of Chapel Hill. She lives in Raleigh, North Carolina, with her husband and children.

V I N T A G E
CONTEMPORARIES

___ **Love Always** by Ann Beattie	$5.95	74418-7
___ **First Love and Other Sorrows** by Harold Brodkey	$5.95	72970-6
___ **The Debut** by Anita Brookner	$5.95	72856-4
___ **Cathedral** by Raymond Carver	$4.95	71281-1
___ **Bop** by Maxine Chernoff	$5.95	75522-7
___ **Dancing Bear** by James Crumley	$5.95	72576-X
___ **One to Count Cadence** by James Crumley	$5.95	73559-5
___ **The Wrong Case** by James Crumley	$5.95	73558-7
___ **The Last Election** by Pete Davies	$6.95	74702-X
___ **A Narrow Time** by Michael Downing	$6.95	75568-5
___ **From Rockaway** by Jill Eisenstadt	$6.95	75761-0
___ **Platitudes** by Trey Ellis	$6.95	75439-5
___ **Days Between Stations** by Steve Erickson	$6.95	74685-6
___ **Rubicon Beach** by Steve Erickson	$6.95	75513-8
___ **A Fan's Notes** by Frederick Exley	$7.95	72915-3
___ **A Piece of My Heart** by Richard Ford	$5.95	72914-5
___ **The Sportswriter** by Richard Ford	$6.95	74325-3
___ **The Ultimate Good Luck** by Richard Ford	$5.95	75089-6
___ **Fat City** by Leonard Gardner	$5.95	74316-4
___ **Ellen Foster** by Kaye Gibbons	$5.95	75757-2
___ **Within Normal Limits** by Todd Grimson	$5.95	74617-1
___ **Airships** by Barry Hannah	$5.95	72913-7
___ **Dancing in the Dark** by Janet Hobhouse	$5.95	72588-3
___ **November** by Janet Hobhouse	$6.95	74665-1
___ **Fiskadoro** by Denis Johnson	$5.95	74367-9
___ **The Stars at Noon** by Denis Johnson	$5.95	75427-1
___ **Asa, as I Knew Him** by Susanna Kaysen	$4.95	74985-5
___ **Lulu Incognito** by Raymond Kennedy	$6.95	75641-X
___ **A Handbook for Visitors From Outer Space** by Kathryn Kramer	$5.95	72989-7
___ **The Chosen Place, the Timeless People** by Paule Marshall	$6.95	72633-2
___ **Suttree** by Cormac McCarthy	$6.95	74145-5
___ **The Bushwhacked Piano** by Thomas McGuane	$5.95	72642-1
___ **Nobody's Angel** by Thomas McGuane	$6.95	74738-0
___ **Something to Be Desired** by Thomas McGuane	$4.95	73156-5
___ **To Skin a Cat** by Thomas McGuane	$5.95	75521-9
___ **Bright Lights, Big City** by Jay McInerney	$5.95	72641-3
___ **Ransom** by Jay McInerney	$5.95	74118-8
___ **River Dogs** by Robert Olmstead	$6.95	74684-8
___ **Soft Water** by Robert Olmstead	$6.95	75752-1
___ **Norwood** by Charles Portis	$5.95	72931-5
___ **Clea & Zeus Divorce** by Emily Prager	$6.95	75591-X
___ **A Visit From the Footbinder** by Emily Prager	$6.95	75592-8
___ **Mohawk** by Richard Russo	$6.95	74409-8
___ **Anywhere But Here** by Mona Simpson	$6.95	75559-6
___ **Carnival for the Gods** by Gladys Swan	$6.95	74330-X
___ **Myra Breckinridge and Myron** by Gore Vidal	$8.95	75444-1
___ **The Car Thief** by Theodore Weesner	$6.95	74097-1
___ **Breaking and Entering** by Joy Williams	$6.95	75773-4
___ **Taking Care** by Joy Williams	$5.95	72912-9

VINTAGE
CONTEMPORARIES

"Today's novels for the readers of today." — <u>VANITY FAIR</u>

"Real literature—originals and important reprints—in attractive, inexpensive paperbacks." — <u>THE LOS ANGELES TIMES</u>

"Prestigious." — <u>THE CHICAGO TRIBUNE</u>

"A very fine collection." — <u>THE CHRISTIAN SCIENCE MONITOR</u>

"Adventurous and worthy." — <u>SATURDAY REVIEW</u>

"If you want to know what's on the cutting edge of American fiction, then these are the books you should be reading."
  — <u>UNITED PRESS INTERNATIONAL</u>

On sale at bookstores everywhere, but if otherwise unavailable, may be ordered from us. You can use this coupon, or phone (800) 638-6460.

Please send me the Vintage Contemporaries books I have checked on the reverse. I am enclosing $ _____ (add $1.00 per copy to cover postage and handling). Send check or money order—no cash or CODs, please. Prices are subject to change without notice.

NAME _____

ADDRESS _____

CITY _____ STATE _____ ZIP _____

Send coupons to:
RANDOM HOUSE, INC., 400 Hahn Road, Westminster, MD 21157
ATTN: ORDER ENTRY DEPARTMENT
Allow at least 4 weeks for delivery.

DATE DUE